GUMBEAUX MAGIC

GUMBEAUX MAGIC

A Novel

(Book 3 of the Gumbeaux Sistahs series)

JAX FREY

Gumbeaux Magic
A Novel

Printed in the United States of America
First Printing 2021

ISBN paperback: 978-1-7331582-2-0

Cover Illustration—*Gumbeaux Sistahs Magic* by Jax Frey

For the true Gumbeaux Sistahs of this world—women everywhere who love life and celebrate and support one another.

To living the Gumbeaux life!

"Magic exists. Who can doubt it, when there
are rainbows and wildflowers,
the music of the wind and the silence of the
stars? Anyone who has loved has been
touched by magic. It is such a simple and such
an extraordinary part of the lives we live."
—Nora Roberts

"And above all, watch with glittering eyes the
whole world around you because
the greatest secrets are always hidden in the
most unlikely places. Those who
don't believe in magic will never find it."
—Roald Dahl

"I am sure there is Magic in everything,
only we have not sense enough
to get hold of it and make it do things for us."
—Frances Hodgson Burnett, *The Secret Garden*

"Magical places are always beautiful and
deserve to be contemplated... Always
Stay on the bridge between the invisible and the visible."
—Paulo Coelho

"Love is already the strongest magic in the world."
—Tera Lynn Childs

"Never, ever stop believing in magic, no matter how old you get.
Because if you keep looking long enough
and don't give up, sooner or
later you're going to find Mary Poppins."
—Steve Kluger

"Life isn't meant to be lived perfectly. . . but
merely to be LIVED. Boldly, wildly,
Beautifully, uncertainly, imperfectly, magically LIVED."
—Mandy Hale

"What do you call a magical bra? An Abracadabra!"
—Unknown

"I think midlife is when the universe gently places her hand upon your shoulders, pulls you close, and whispers in your ear: I'm not screwing around. It's time. All of this pretending and performing these coping mechanisms that you've developed to protect yourself from feeling inadequate and getting hurt—has to go. Your armor is preventing you from growing into your gifts. I understand that you needed these protections when you were small. I understand that you believed your armor could help you secure all of the things you needed to feel worthy of love and belonging, but you're still searching and you're more lost than ever. Time is growing short. There are unexplored adventures ahead of you. You can't live the rest of your life worried about what other people think. You were born worthy of love and belonging. Courage and daring are coursing through you. You were made to live and love with your whole heart.

It's time to show up and be seen."

—Brene' Brown

Used with permission

LIST OF CHARACTERS

Original Gumbeaux Sistahs:

Judith Lafferty – artist, single, and co-owner along with Dawn Berard of The Gumbeaux Sistahs Gallery

Dawn Berard – co-owner of The Gumbeaux Sistahs Gallery and owner of family business Berard Accounting. Was married to Dan Berard, now widowed.

Lola Broussard – Landscaper, lawyer, activist, best friends with Dawn and married twice to same man, Bud Broussard

Bea Walker – retired, widow, unofficial leader of the Gumbeaux Sistahs, lay minister with Episcopal Church, co-creator of the Friendship Bench

Helen Hoffmann – owner of Body Workings Essential Oils Company, widow, co-creator of the Friendship Bench

Additional Gumbeaux Sistahs

Bitsy Rogers – newly added Gumbeaux Sistah, Director of Covington Art Museum

Trinity Hebert – newly added Gumbeaux Sistah and Dawn's little sister, owner of Royal Gala Art Gallery in New Orleans. Married to Harry Hebert, owner of River Oil Company

Other Characters

Bud Broussard – married twice to Lola Broussard and owner of Broussard Nursery

Marty LeBlanc – Judith's boyfriend, retired architect, now woodworker

Cooper Landry – Helen's foster child, student

Andre Dupre – Cooper's abusive stepfather

Lillian Deslattes – Gumbeaux Sistah nemesis, Chairwoman of the board at Covington Art Museum, married to Jack Deslattes, retired. The Deslattes own large real estate firm - Magnolia Real Estate

Zoe Abadie – Dawn's Granddaughter, student

Pauline Landry – former streetwalker with pink hair

Benny Williams – Pauline's pimp

Brenda Beckham – Marty's assistant in his woodworking business

"Man, I just love funeral potatoes!"
He looked up and asked his creator,
"Lord, do they have those in Heaven?
Never mind, of course they do!"
—Dan Berard

PROLOGUE

Dan Berard lay quietly in his coffin in his best, tailored suit with the blue power tie. His wife, Dawn, sat in the first pew of Grace Episcopal Church in Covington, Louisiana. On either side sat her daughters, Clair and Jennifer. All three women wept softly as Reverend Jim said kind and deserved words about the deceased. "Dan was a good husband, father, friend, parishioner, philanthropist, and volunteer. He will be greatly missed by the parish and by everyone who knew him."

In his coffin, Dan grinned to himself thinking, "Now that's the stuff. I hope they say a lot more just like that." Then something else occurred to him, "Shoot, I just realized that I'm gonna miss the reception back at the house and I'll bet someone will bring funeral potatoes. Man, I just love funeral potatoes!" He looked up and asked his creator, "Lord, do they have those in Heaven? Never mind, of course they do!"

Dawn, meanwhile, felt a fresh rush of grief and hot tears and then the comforting touch of several hands on her shoulders from the pew behind her.

Her best friends, Lola, Bea, Helen, Judith, Bitsy, and Trinity, stood by to help her get through the terrible day. They called themselves the Gumbeaux Sistahs because of their love of great gumbo, their appreciation of Cajun culture, and because, while most of them were not officially related, they were sisters in spirit. Today, their hearts went out to their sister who had lost her husband of over thirty years to cancer. Her tears were theirs. They had all known and loved Dan too.

Meanwhile, back at the coffin, Dan, whose soul was at this point midway between heaven and earth, thought, "Dawn, my girl, you're on your own now, but I'll try somehow to check on you. And don't worry, I'll wait for you, and I'll be with you again someday. But take your time. There's no hurry, and I'm sure you'll have lots of adventures before it's time for you to jump ship. Meanwhile, do me proud with that money I left in our donation fund. Find some worthy local cause that calls to your heart and could use that thirty-thousand dollars. I know I can count on you." His thoughts turned to his dear wife and how she was now on her own without his steadying influence to balance her out. Dawn—set loose upon the world. He rolled his spirit eyes and look heavenward, "Lord, help them all now!"

"You never know when you'll need a green and purple tutu and matching shoes."
—Trinity

CHAPTER 1

THREE MONTHS LATER

Trinity, Dawn's younger sister by six years, used the tape gun to pack up another moving box of Harry's belongings. Her husband of ten years had moved out, and she was putting together boxes of his belongings that still needed to be cleared out.

"Oh, Harry," she thought sadly with a sharp jab at her heart, a frequent occurrence these days. She had grown used to and dependent on him and, truth be told, his bottomless checkbook from the River Oil Company that he owned. But she had been genuinely fond of him too.

Even so, she thought of the red flags that went up when they were dating. She had not known that he was already married. She had no idea that he already had a wife and kids when he got down on one knee and proposed to her. It had been a bombshell when he explained that he was in the middle of a divorce and had to "tie up some loose ends" before they could tie their own knot. Four months later, they had stood up before a priest and friends and promised their forever love. At least she had. Apparently, he had only promised it till he met a blonde thirty-five-year-old gold digger named Eileen.

A friend of Trinity's had texted her a picture of Eileen and Harry at a dark bar named The Maxx out in Metairie, Louisiana. The couple had a lip lock going in the photo that could have won an

Olympic competition. But it only spelled out one thing to Trinity and for their marriage.

Of course, it broke her heart. It also made her wonder, and not for the first time, if Harry's claims were true that he was already in the process of divorcing his wife before he had met Trinity. The old saying, "Once a cheater, always a cheater," rang through her brain about once every five minutes these days. She thought it was probably a wonder they had stayed married as long as they had.

Still, she would miss him. At least that part of him that was cute, fun, flirty, and rich. Together they owned their French Quarter apartment in New Orleans, and he was walking away, leaving it to her. That made sense since her business, The Royal Gala Art Gallery, was on the floor below their apartment. The gallery did well financially, so she would be fine with her own money, just not crazy-rich anymore if she didn't get anything in the divorce beyond the apartment. She didn't expect to get much though. Harry had insisted on a pretty solid prenup.

She walked around the apartment looking for more of Harry's odds and ends that he might have missed. She checked in their bedroom and bathroom and then moved on to the door in the hall to what she called her Costume Room. Opening the door, she scanned the mirror-lined walls and racks upon racks of wigs, sparkly jewelry, boas, glittery shoes, and other costume pieces. She realized that there was nothing of Harry's in this room. It was all hers and reflected her personality perfectly.

She caught her reflection in one of the large mirrors and studied it for a moment. Her hand went to her soft brown, highlighted hair cut in a perfect, elegant bob. Her figure was still good and curvy. She wasn't quite as tall as her sister, Dawn, but while Dawn could look intimidatingly large, Trinity looked shapely. "Harry, you're such a halfwit," she thought miserably.

A thought occurred to her as she was cleaning out Harry's stuff, *"Hmm, maybe I should get rid of some of my stuff too while I'm cleaning up. There's an awful lot in here—maybe it's too much."* It took her only one beat before she laughed and said out loud, "Who am I kidding? There's no such thing as too much! You never know when you'll need a green and purple tutu and matching shoes." Those colors suddenly reminded her of an invitation that had arrived in the mail the day before. She hurried to the living room where the invite still sat waiting on a side table for her RSVP. It was addressed only to Trinity, and not to her and Harry, which she took as a good sign. It read:

Come Ring in the Mardi Gras Season
At Rocky Breaux's place
Dress: Like your favorite Hooker!
Saturday, January 9th. 8 P.M. till-?
420 Bourbon St.
RSVP

Rocky Breaux had been her best friend back in the small town of Breaux Bridge, Louisiana, where they had grown up. When Trinity's mother died, Rocky had been like his name—a solid rock for her. He gave her someone to turn to besides her loving big sister, Dawn, who had basically raised Trinity and her other siblings for the remainder of their childhood. She loved Rocky like a brother. Now he lived in the French Quarter not far from Trinity, and he was known for his outrageous parties. This one sounded like a good one.

Trinity had hesitated when the invitation first arrived the day before. At first, she thought she had too much to do to attend the party—running her busy gallery and clearing her apartment of signs that Harry had ever lived there. She wondered, *"Am I really in the mood, and do I have the energy to show up in full style and regalia? I know that Rocky is expecting this of me."*

She quickly closed her eyes and did a fast examination of her body and spirit as if she was on an operating table. *"All parts are accounted for – except part of my heart is missing,"* she thought. *"But I'm still me,"* she suddenly realized with relief. Her personality and psyche existed independently of her marriage. She was Trinity Hebert—New Orleans socialite extraordinaire—the one and only. The thought made her laugh out loud, mostly because she knew it was true.

Still smiling, she dialed Rocky's number. When he picked up, she said simply, "I'll be there."

"Oh my gravy, girl! Of course you will! It wouldn't be a party without my Trinity."

"It's because you know women can't resist the funky, sex-god look!"
—Judith

CHAPTER 2

Judith Lafferty was in her boyfriend Marty's workshop in his backyard. The large wooden beams and rusty tin roof of the shop made for an authentic, craftsman atmosphere. And Marty LeBlanc was quite a craftsman. The two of them had come together as a couple just a year before and were still going strong. He was a recent retiree from his architectural business and had since taken an interest in woodworking. His workshop was filled with finished projects—chairs, dressers, night tables, cutting boards, and even some wooden toys, along with several unfinished items that he was working on today.

Judith was helping him by sanding down a dresser. She wore a pair of soft jeans that fit her snugly along with an old plaid shirt of Marty's that she had confiscated for such activities. She had pulled her shoulder-length, blonde hair back with a scrunchy so she could concentrate on the job without it swinging in her face. The couple worked quietly as the radio played old rock-and-roll tunes. Judith's mind was wandering as her gaze fell softly on the lovely wooden items lining the walls of the building. In her mind's eye, the old workshop was inspiring, and she was envisioning a new painting she would like to create with a rustic wood background. It would feature the Gumbeaux Sistahs figures that she loved to paint. She pictured the women playing Cajun instruments like the accordion, the fiddle, and the banjo in an old, funky setting like the workshop. She decided she would start the new piece that very afternoon so she could get it into her gallery by the following week.

Almost two years ago, she and Dawn Berard had opened a joint venture business called the Gumbeaux Sistahs Gallery. It was located in downtown Covington, Louisiana, and offered Judith's paintings and gift items as well as the work of a few other local, talented artists. The gallery sold coffee and dessert as well, making it as much a community gathering spot as a gallery. Regulars could be found most days sitting at one of the little tables sipping their coffee, eating pastries, and meeting their friends.

She was brought suddenly out of her reverie when she felt Marty's hand touching her shoulder. "Where'd you go?" he asked with a slight smile. "You were sanding so hard in your daydream that I thought you were going to work your way clear down to the cement floor."

Judith laughed and reached up to push back a bit of Marty's hair that was threatening to land in front of his eyes. He was wearing his thick hair longer than he used to, a symbol of how he was embracing his new artistic lifestyle. It was a complete change from his former corporate life. Now he was the personification of a silver-haired, bohemian artist. She liked to tease him. "I know why you've taken up woodworking and the longer hair, Marty. It's because you know that women can't resist the funky, sex-god look."

"Yep—that's what I was going for, alright. It's a tough job, but someone's gotta do it." He laughed good-naturedly.

They had met just a year before, but it felt like they had known each other forever. Marty was a widower, and Judith was divorced from her second husband years ago. She had been convinced that she was done with romance until Marty showed up in the gallery one day, and the rest was, so far, so amazing.

"After this last dresser is done, I'm going to pack up the trailer and drive up to Baton Rouge this weekend for that arts and crafts show I told you about. It's a big event and a big deal for me. And as you know, it's my first show. My first foray into the outdoor show business. I sure hope this stuff sells," he said, looking around with a worried frown.

"You've just got artist angst, Marty," she said confidently. "Every artist goes through it. But listen to me, Marty Leblanc. You've got so much talent at this. You were a talented architect, and so it's not at all fair that you'd be a talented woodworker too, but such is life." She laughed and hugged him around his middle.

"Wish you could come with me," he said hopefully, even though they had already had this conversation.

"I promise that I'll go with you another time. I just can't make this one. The gallery has an art opening for the beginning of Mardi Gras season this weekend. Dawn would kill me if I wasn't there."

"Well, wish me luck then."

"Good luck, my dear, but you won't need it—wait and see. And take care of yourself, OK? Ever since Dawn's husband, Dan, passed, I've been paranoid. Think about it—Bea and Helen are already widows, and now so is Dawn. And Trinity is going through a divorce. The Gumbeaux Sistahs' men are dropping like flies. It worries me."

"Don't worry about me, Judith. You're stuck with me for a long time. You'll probably come to regret it," he smiled at her.

She laughed as she washed her hands at the sink. "I doubt that, but listen, I've got to run now. I've got a painting that I'm just itching to get to."

As she was walking out of the door, Brenda Beckham, Marty's assistant, walked in. She was in her early forties, slim, tanned, and pretty with her long, blond, swinging hair. Marty had hired her part-time to help with the bookkeeping and to help out with scheduling and office work. "Oh, hello, Judith." Then she called out, "Marty, I've got to ask you about these receipts—not sure what they're for."

"Well, come on in and let's take a look," he said.

Judith left them with their heads together looking at the receipts and felt a little gnawing of discomfort. But she quickly dismissed it, thinking, *"Nah. Marty's one of the good ones."* But she didn't know Brenda. She hoped Brenda was one of the good ones too.

“Don’t worry. You’ll get our damned quota.”
—Pauline

CHAPTER 3

Rocky greeted Trinity at his front door wearing a gold, glittery mini skirt and purple boa and carrying a King Cake martini, complete with a green and purple sugared rim, which he placed immediately into her outstretched hand. She was always grateful for his zaniness—and his alcohol. She loved his unbridled expressiveness. As for the martini, after the week she'd had cleaning away the last vestiges of Harry, she planned on having two or three more.

"Oh my gravy! I am so glad you came. I've been meaning to come over all week and help you with the house, but I just couldn't get away."

"Rocky, I'm so glad I came too. I needed a party to take my mind off things. And this martini—wow! As for the house, I've cleaned out Harry's stuff, but come on over next week some afternoon. I'd like to re-arrange the furniture, so the place reminds me less of him."

"You got it, girl. I'll come over, but for now, let's just bend our elbows a lot tonight. C'mon, I've got new fabulous people for you to meet."

As usual, Rocky's parties involved many crazy drinking games with names like Fuzzy Duck or Most Likely To. Of course, there was always fabulous food he had made himself, since he was a renowned local chef. One could also expect lots of beautiful people to attend and a great deal of dancing. Trinity was not the only "hooker" wearing fishnet stockings that night, but she was the only one wearing a pair of sunglasses that lit up and spelled *S-L-U-T* across the top. She had found them in a vintage store on Bourbon Street. It was a treasure, and she got many laughing compliments on her "tastefulness." Rocky swore he was going to steal them.

As fun as it was, after a few hours of partying, Trinity was feeling the wear of her terrible week. A little after midnight found Trinity feeling heavy in the eyelids. She knew she had had enough. She kissed her dear friend goodbye at the door and declined his many offers of walking her the two blocks back to her house. "It's early yet on Bourbon Street," she told him. "And there's plenty of people out still. I'll be fine, Rocky."

"OK," he said reluctantly. "But text me the minute you walk in the door or when you are picked up by your first 'John' on your way home!" He giggled, pointing to her *S-L-U-T* glasses.

"What do you mean—my first?" she teased, looking over one shoulder. She waved goodbye to her old friend.

"Seriously, though!" he called. "I'll be waiting for your text."

She got down to the next corner and walked by a group of three, rough-looking women standing on the corner. There was one man among them talking loudly. His tone made Trinity look up in alarm. He didn't seem to realize that Trinity was behind him as he yelled angrily in one woman's face, "Listen to me, you lazy cow. You got a quota to make. You make it, Pauline, or I'll make you wish you had, you got me?" He lifted his fist up to the woman's face in a warning.

The woman named Pauline was not young—somewhere in her forties probably, but with her harsh makeup in the garish streetlight, she looked fiftyish. Her skirt was even shorter than Rocky's had been, and she wore a tiny, low-cut, pink halter top and five-inch heels. "I get it, Benny. I get it." She said, obviously fearful and resentful of the man. "Don't worry. You'll get your damned *quota*." She said the last word in a mocking tone.

"*Oh boy*," thought Trinity, "*This doesn't look good. I'd better get the heck out of here*." She swung her handbag over her shoulder firmly and hurried past them just as the man turned and saw her.

"What the hell are you doing here? Are you one of Larry's girls?" He looked her up and down and added, "If so, I feel sorry for Larry!" He started to roar with laughter but stopped suddenly and said angrily, "Get off this corner! You know this is my corner."

Startled, Trinity walked faster, and the man turned and stalked angrily up the street in the opposite direction. Just then, she heard a voice behind her, "Hey, girl! Wait up!"

Trinity glanced behind her and was surprised to see the woman named Pauline walking fast towards her with her hand out, holding something.

"*Oh hell in a basket*," thought Trinity in panic, "*Is that a gun? Is she coming to rob me?*"

The woman caught up to her and said, "Hey, you move pretty fast for an old Lady! Where you working at tonight?"

Trinity just whispered softly with fright, "Working?"

"Talk louder, will you? If a man asks you to party with him, how's he gonna hear you when you say 'show me your money, sugar!'" She cackled loudly.

Trinity could only stare at her.

"Oh, so you don't feel like talking to Pauline? Well, that's OK, I was just bringing you this."

Trinity looked at the woman's hand, the one she originally thought held a gun, and recognized her cell phone.

"Yeah, you dropped it back there. Can't do no business these days without it."

Trinity was overwhelmed with relief at seeing that it was not a gun. She looked up straight into the eyes of the stranger dressed in very little clothing, "Oh!" she said, "Thank you! That was so kind of you."

"Yeah, well," the woman said, laughing. "That's me. Heart of gold and all that."

Trinity took the phone and started to thank the woman again when bright lights and a loud siren split the night, turning her into a deer in headlights. *"What is this? What now?"* she thought, horrified.

"Oh shoot," said Pauline, "Here we go again."

"Hey, you two," yelled a man's voice. "Police! Get yourselves over here with these other girls and get up against the wall."

**“Ooh, she owns an art gallery! And I’m a heart surgeon.
Marcy, I bet you’s the Queen of France!
—Sheila**

CHAPTER 4

Rocky was picking up empty glasses and paper plates in his apartment when his phone rang. Seeing who it was, he answered, "Hey, you were supposed to text me when you got home. I was worried! Are you alright?"

As he listened, his eyes grew large, and he opened his mouth in a big O and said, "Oh my gravy, girl! I was only kidding when I said you should pick up a John! Where are you?" His face took on a horrified expression, "What?" he screamed. "OK, hold tight, Trinity. I'll call my lawyer, and we'll have you out before you know it." He stopped and then giggled, "I'll have you back out on the streets again before you can say shake your money maker!"

He hung up and dialed the number for Jack Lance, who had luckily just been at the party half hour before. "Hope you're not home yet, Jack. Turn that car around and meet me at Central Lockup!"

Trinity hung up the phone and was led back to the cell she shared with the three other women with whom she had been arrested. She sat down on a bench feeling frightened and exhausted and tried to look invisible. The other women were laughing raucously, all looking at her.

"What are you supposed to be?" one of them asked. Then, "Don't you know you're too old, girl? Who'd pay for your raggedly old ass?"

"Yeah, you gotta be starting to think about retirement, grandma."

One of the women who returned her cell phone to her came and sat down next to Trinity.

"Don't mind them old whores," she said. "My name is Pauline, sugar. What's yours?"

"I'm Trinity. I'm not supposed to be here, Pauline."

"Oh, she's not supposed to be here, Pauline," mimicked one of the other women.

"Shut up, dumb ass. Anybody with a brain can see she's not supposed to be here." She turned back to Trinity and looked her up and down. "Of course, you are dressed the part. What's up with that?"

"I was coming from a party," explained Trinity, her eyes closed in exhaustion. "Everyone at the party was dressed like this."

"Oh man! I'm gonna have to remember that one next time the cops pick us up," laughed Pauline. "What do you do, Trinity? You live around the French Quarter?"

"Yes, I do, near where they picked us up, actually. I own the Royal Gala Art Gallery on Royal Street."

One of the other women called out, "Ooh, she owns an art gallery! And I'm a heart surgeon. Marcy, I bet you's the Queen of France!"

"France don't have no queen, idiot," said Pauline. "Just leave her alone, OK? You'd better start thinking about what we're gonna tell Benny when he bails us out. Ain't nobody around here making their quota tonight."

She turned back to Trinity, "You got somebody coming for you?"

"Yes," said Trinity. "They should be here before too long. It's just a terrible mistake, is all."

"Ain't it always!" laughed Sheila.

"Look, Trinity, you just stick with me. These idiots will leave you alone, and Benny is gonna kill us all anyways when he gets here," said Pauline.

"Sounds like you need to get the heck away from Benny, Pauline," said Trinity, looking at the other woman carefully for the first time. Why hadn't she noticed before that the woman had pink hair?

"That's easier said than done," whispered Pauline, looking away.

They were quiet together for a moment, settling down to wait for someone to bail them out.

Before too long, a commotion from the front office got their attention, and Rocky Breaux and his lawyer were led to their cell by an officer. The lawyer was shouting, "This is Mrs. Trinity Hebert, owner of the Royal Gala Art Gallery and wife of Harry Hebert, owner of River Oil Company, perhaps you've heard of it? Does she look like a streetwalker to you?"

"Well, actually, she kind of does," answered the policeman, calmly staring at Trinity's sunglasses that she had pushed on top of her head that spelled out *S-L-U-T*.

"Oh my gravy—it's just a party costume! This is New Orleans, for heaven's sake! We wear costumes here sometimes; in case you hadn't noticed. She was at my party earlier tonight, so I can tell you for sure, she's not a tart!"

The other women snickered at Rocky, "He called us tarts–I kinda like that. Hey, I'm a poptart!"

The policeman protested, "But she was with these women. Were they at the party too?"

Sheila spoke up immediately, "Yes, we were, officer." Then she whispered to Rocky, "Say yes, little man. Say yes, and I'll make it worth your while."

"You're barking up the wrong tree, I'm afraid," Rocky whispered back, then shrugged.

"Officer, she was just walking by us when you picked us up," said Pauline, "She's not with us. It was just terrible timing for her."

The police officer opened the cell and said apologetically, "Come on out, Miss Hebert. The department is sorry about this mistake, but surely you can understand how this happened."

Rocky draped a sweater he had brought from the house around Trinity's shoulders and led her to the door.

Pauline called out, "Take care, Miss Trinity."

Trinity turned back, feeling sad for the woman who had helped her, "You too, Pauline. Thanks for your kindness."

"Mess is mess. Marie Kondo would have a field day in here."
—Judith

CHAPTER 5

Judith let herself into the front door of her cottage, juggling her purse, keys, a soy latte, and a bag of groceries while trying not to step on her little pug. Lucy was two years old but still puppyish and overjoyed to see her.

"Hey, Lucy-girl!" said Judith, who was just as happy to see her crazy, heart-stealing, little dog. They had found each other a little over a year ago when the pug showed up in her front yard. After numerous attempts to find its owner, Judith finally gave up and gave in to the surprising love and devotion she had for Lucy.

She walked through the house and down the hall with the pup trailing happily behind her. She carefully dodged the numerous paintings and art supplies that lined the walls and filled every corner of the house these days. She got to the kitchen and looked for a place to put the groceries down but found that even the island was covered with a stack of painted watercolors. She gave up and put the bag down on the floor and looked around.

"How did it get this bad?" she groaned out loud.

She headed back through the house and found that there was not a single room that didn't store paintings. Plus, there was a load of them in her studio. It was not a large house in the first place. And since she had opened the Gumbeaux Sistahs Gallery with Dawn, she'd had to clear out many of her paintings from the studio to make room for her to paint. They just seemed to be cloning—or breeding.

Most of the work was older paintings that had not sold or were not appropriate for the new gallery in some way, or they were just not quite up to Judith's current level of artistry. She always thought that she would go back to them someday and take another stab at the work to see if she could redeem them and bring them up to her standards. They weren't bad or far off the mark, but they were not quite up to snuff. Unfortunately, she just had not found the time to make that happen, what with the gallery taking off and her time spent with Marty and her friends, the Gumbeaux Sistahs. So, the house was overflowing with art.

"*I suppose this might sound like a good problem to have to some people*," thought Judith with a sigh, "*But mess is mess. Marie Kondo would have a field day in here.*"

She sighed again and went back to putting away the groceries which contained all the makings of a good gumbo. The Sistahs were meeting at her place in a couple of days, and she wanted to get started on the cooking. She loved getting together with her friends, but at this point, with all her mess, she did not know where she would even put them.

She turned to Lucy and chuckled, "They might just have to sit on you, Lucy."

Lucy gave her an outraged look and thought, *Ha! They are more likely to sit on you. They know that I'll bite them in the butt!*

“Actually, you sound just like Dawn.”
—Bea

CHAPTER 6

Bea was to begin her first duties as a lay minister connected with Grace Episcopal Church. As such, she was encouraged to make visits to home-bound parishioners and hospital patients to offer what comfort she could.

"Well, Bea," said Helen, as they talked on the phone that morning. Helen was a Gumbeaux Sistah too and best friends with Bea for many years. "Are you ready for your first day? And, more importantly, are they ready for you?" She laughed because she knew that Bea was a strong, determined woman—a force of nature. You would never know it to look at her petite five-foot-four self that always sported a cute, little straw hat pulled over her salt-and-pepper hair.

For the last six months, Bea had undergone training in the lay ministry program. The training was an extension of the church, and Bea had originally signed up for it because she thought it would help with their project, the Friendship Bench. The project was the brainchild of Bea and Helen, and it entailed taking turns sitting and talking with various people on the three benches they had set up in different locations. One was in a Covington park, one in Abita Springs, and one in front of the Gumbeaux Sistahs Gallery. People were welcome to take turns sitting on a bench with a Friend, usually Bea or Helen, and talking about anything they wanted. Sometimes they discussed the difficulties of their lives, but sometimes they were just lonely and wanted someone to talk to about the weather or their recipe for barbecued shrimp. Helen and Bea were the only two Friends at first, but now they had several volunteers to help. People found out about the benches by word of mouth only, but that word was spreading, and they were getting ready to add a new bench on the side of the church. More volunteers were showing up from the church itself to come and sit with people. The bench was a success before it even existed. Bea, Helen, and many others considered it their personal ministry.

But today, Bea was going to step up her game. She was due to spend three hours a week at the hospital, visiting rooms on the second floor in the trauma ward, offering what comfort she could.

"Ready or not, here I come," said Bea, still talking on the phone with Helen while adding a colorful scarf to her ensemble, hoping that she looked cheerful.

"Those patients won't know what hit 'em," said Helen, then she back-tracked, "Oh wait, they're already in the trauma ward, so poor choice of words, I guess."

Bea picked up her keys and purse, "You're incorrigible, dear. Actually, you sound just like Dawn. Ok, I'm off. I'll check in with your later."

She was only five minutes from the hospital, and she pulled into the parking lot right on time. The nurses were busy but quickly showed Bea a group of rooms she should visit. Taking a deep breath, she thought, *"OK, here goes something, I hope."*

She stepped into a room where a sleeping older gentleman lay with tubes and wires attached every which way. She sat in a chair by his side and waited to see if he would awaken. When he did not, she lightly picked up his hand and said a prayer for him. Then she laid one of her business cards that she'd had printed on his bedside table that read:

Bea Walker
If you need a friend to talk to,
email me at:
beaw@friendshipbench.com
Meanwhile I'll pray for you.

She slipped out of the room and moved on. When she entered the semi-darkness of the next room, she saw a slender woman with dark hair lying on her side, facing away from the door. Bea could tell that the woman was crying softly to herself. She took a deep breath and prepared to extend her hand in friendship, saying softly, "Good morning. My name is Bea Walker from Grace Episcopal Church, and if you'd like, I can sit with you for a little while. I'm just here to check on how you are."

When she went around to the other side of the bed, she stopped short and looked closer.

The woman with dark bruises on her face looked up at her visitor and let out a moan, "Oh, now that's just what I freakin' need! If it isn't one of those damned Gumbeaux Sistahs!"

Bea gasped, "Lillian Deslattes!"

"Jack? Where is Jack?"
—Lillian

CHAPTER 7

Lillian was beat to pieces from the car accident she had been in two days prior. She and her husband Jack had been driving home from a weekend in Natchez, Mississippi when it happened. It had been such a lovely weekend, too—mostly. The couple had needed a getaway and some time alone after so many years together. The last few had been particularly trying due to infidelities—both hers and his. They were making an attempt to recover from it. Lillian had the idea that a little romantic weekend, strolling along the bluffs overlooking the Mississippi River, drinking margaritas poolside, and dining at restaurants in beautiful antebellum homes might reignite a spark that had undoubtedly been there when they were young. It seemed to be working too. They had shared laughter and easy times over the weekend, especially that last morning at their breakfast table in their hotel. Reaching for the cream, Jack had spilled his coffee so disastrously that they both had French toast full of brown liquid. First Jack chuckled, and then Lillian guffawed, and before long, they were holding onto each other with laughter. Tears were streaming down their cheeks as if they were college students again and not the elegant couple who owned St. Tammany Parish's premiere real estate company.

When they checked out of the hotel, they were still in a good mood. They shared more laughs in the car, remembering the disastrous spill. That mood lasted until, driving past McComb, something came over Jack. Lillian could sense it immediately. She could feel the iciness in the car taking over and felt helpless to stop it. She knew what it was, and Jack proved it when he finally asked her, "Did you laugh like that when you were with your boy-toy Thomas?"

Even though they both were indiscreet simultaneously, Jack could not seem to get over it and let it be, as Lillian mostly had. She felt she had to or lose the marriage. She wished Jack felt the same way, but he still brought it up occasionally. They had even been to counseling, trying to talk it through. Lillian had found it enormously helpful. Apparently, Jack had not.

Lillian hated when Jack was angry in the car. He was a fast, aggressive driver to begin with, passing everything he could and veering around big trucks while Lillian held her breath.

The changeover from Highway 55 to Interstate 12 near Hammond was always tricky. It was a large interstate with people entering and exiting at the same time. Lillian saw the big truck in the right lane barreling up behind them before Jack did.

"Watch out, Jack," she said tensely.

By this time, Jack's impatience and anger had reached a dangerous level, and he was not in the mood to take orders from Lillian. Recklessly, he pulled into the left lane of the interstate, and seconds later, the truck backended them doing seventy-five. It was a horrendous wreck.

At least that was what they told Lillian when she woke up in St. Tammany Hospital. She did not remember the accident at all. She only remembered how angry Jack had been in the car and how sad she had felt over their ruined weekend. She was sadder still over the state of the marriage. She loved Jack but did not see how they would get past their regrettable peccadillos.

But now, she also remembered the doctor's words, "Lillian, you're in the hospital, and you've been in an accident. You have a fractured leg, and we had to operate and insert pins to save your ability to walk. Your arm is broken, and that's why it's in a cast. Plus, you've suffered a concussion."

"Jack? Where is Jack?" was all she asked.

"I'm afraid your husband is in intensive care. He was hurt very badly in the accident. He suffered a skull fracture. We are doing everything we can for him."

That was two days ago, and not much had changed. Lillian had not even been able to see Jack yet because she could not move out of bed herself. She was scared, in pain, alone, and miserable. And now she had one of her old nemeses, a Gumbeaux Sistah, in her room. If she were not so beaten up, she might have hurled a bedpan across the room.

"Lillian, what are you doing here? What happened to you?" asked Bea, disbelieving.

Lillian stared daggers at Bea, then answered in a tight voice, "Oh, don't pretend to be nice to me, Bea Walker. I know you just can't wait to go back and tell your so-called sistahs that I'm laid up here. They'll probably throw a party."

"No, dear," answered Bea quietly. "That, of course, is not true. I'm shocked to find you here and can't believe that you're so hurt."

Lillian closed her eyes for a second, already tired from the ordeal of talking, "It was a car accident, and my husband is in the ICU."

"Oh no," said Bea, "I'm so sorry, dear. How are you feeling?"

"I feel like hell. How do you think I feel?" Tears sprang into Lillian's eyes, and the pain felt worse by the second. Not only was she in terrible pain, but she also hated for anyone to see her look so awful. She was always known for her sharp, elegant outfits and her black hair always pulled into a chic chignon.

"Try to calm yourself just a little, Lillian. You getting upset is not going to help anything. If my being here upsets you, I'll go. But I'll pray for you, and if there's anything I can do for you, please tell me."

Lillian looked around miserably. Her brother and children had visited the day before and said they were coming back today sometime, but she felt completely alone at the moment in all this, and she was so worried about Jack.

Bea was heading towards the door, and Lillian said desperately, "Wait! Can you see if you can find out anything more about Jack? I have the feeling they are keeping things from me, but I need to know. Maybe they'll tell you."

Bea saw the desperation in the other women's eyes and nodded, "I'll see if they will tell me, Lillian. I'll be back."

As she left the room, Bea felt pity for this woman well up in her chest, and she shook her head as tears threatened to spill over. She blinked them back, thinking, *"Life is so full of irony."* She remembered the harsh history she and the sistahs had with Lillian, who used to be Judith's boss at the Covington Art Museum. Lillian had been Chairwoman of the board and held her power over every other board member and its employees like a sword. Everyone had been afraid of the sharp tongue that she had never hesitated to use. Judith had been manager of the museum for ten years when Lillian had plotted to oust her and replace her with her boyfriend of that time, a young man named Thomas McCann. When she finally succeeded in getting Judith fired unfairly, the sistahs had stepped in and turned the tables on Lillian. Thomas ended up in jail for theft, Lillian lost credibility at the museum, and her husband had discovered her infidelity. In the end, Bitsy got promoted to Director, and Judith opened the Gumbeaux Sistahs Gallery with Dawn, fulfilling a life-long dream of making her living by creating art.

Of course, Lillian had not taken it well at all. Even though she had kept her seat on the board, she had lost her iron-grip power over them. Plus, her marriage had suffered terribly. She was not exactly one to forgive and forget either. Every time she had encountered one of the sistahs—and in their small town, that was easy to do—she could swear she tasted sulfur in her mouth because, let's face it, she had been deservedly burned.

"And now, just when I'm completely helpless, not to mention in terrible pain, who should end up at my bedside? None other than the unofficial leader of the Sistahs, Bea Walker, who says she wants to pray for me! I swear I'd rather fracture another leg than deal with her!"

“How can I live though this?
What can I do to make myself even want to?”
—Dawn

CHAPTER 8

Dawn sat on the bed in her dark bedroom. Even though the house was empty except for herself, she closed the doors, locked them, and pulled the shades. Not only did she want no one to see her, but she wanted the entire universe to stay at bay as well. Her world had stopped in its tracks and all she felt was pain.

When the crying and heartache over Dan's loss got too awful to bear, as it did several times a day, she wanted to keep it strictly to herself. Not even her best friend Lola was allowed to witness this degree of grief.

Tears streamed down her cheeks in sheets, soaking the tissues she replenished every couple of minutes. She was sobbing so hard that her whole body shook. She did not feel physical pain, but she was in agony, nonetheless. If someone had broken into the house and stabbed her with a very dull, jagged knife, it would not hurt worse than this.

Her mind, which was as dull as dirt these days, flitted desperately from one thought to another. *"How can I live though this? What can I do to make myself even want to?"*

The days since the funeral had been filled with a gut-wrenching sadness. She kept having moments of forgetfulness where she expected to turn the corner in a room to find her husband at the breakfast table reading the morning headlines, or in the bathroom taking a shower, or to come in from the garden any second. Then she would remember and the disbelief, the horror would set in all over again. So deep was the grief that sat on her chest, she thought it might crush her.

Even though theirs had been a loving marriage she couldn't help but remember all the times when she could have been kinder to him. Why hadn't she been kinder? Would it have killed her? She would end her own life for another chance to be kind to him. Just one more chance.

There is nothing more powerful than love and its loss is equally powerful. Dawn wished that she could just stop breathing. Just stop everything and be with Dan again.

Then she remembered something a neighbor, an older widow lady, had told her. She said to think of the grief and sadness as the waves of the ocean. Right now, she was trying to walk in the deep water and the waves are crashing down upon her, pushing her around, exhausting and almost drowning her. But as time goes by, she will walk in the water a little closer to shore. The waves will still be rough and occasionally knock her over and tire her out, but she can keep walking with some effort. But then after some more time passes, she will walk even closer to shore and her legs and will become stronger and accustomed to the water, and it will feel natural to her. Eventually, she will be able to walk onto the shore, but the thing is, she will always feel those waves, even if they are tiny, coming up to meet her once in a while because she will never forget what has happened. It is a part of who she is now. But she will be able to live her life fully without the searing pain and go on. She only has to keep walking.

Dawn tried to think of those words now in her dark bedroom.

She dried her eyes and stood up knowing that the waves would come for her again soon. But for right now, right this moment, she would keep walking.

“Don’t I clean up good?”
—Pauline

CHAPTER 9

Trinity was in her art gallery going over the day's receipts. She had been taking it easy the last couple of days, still shaken from her arrest and rescue. She was also recovering from the deluge of teasing she had taken from her sister, Dawn, when she told her what had happened.

"If you needed money, Trin, you should have just come to me. After all, what can you make from selling your body these days? Five dollars?" Dawn taunted her unmercifully.

Trinity gave a deep sigh as she went through the paperwork. Then, she heard the front door open behind her. Turning to greet the customer, she stopped cold. The woman looked familiar, but she did not recognize her at first. She wore a bright pink, wrap-around dress with matching shoes, hat—and hair. It was a walking billboard for something, but Trinity wasn't sure what. She did a double take, and then it hit her.

"Miss Trinity?" said the woman, her head held high, "I've come to ask you for a job."

Trinity recognized one of the women she had been arrested with. She said, "Oh!" Then she recovered from the shock, "Pauline, is that you?"

"Yes, ma'am. I don't blame you for not recognizing me. Don't I clean up good?" she asked.

"Yes, indeed you do!" said Trinity because, in spite of the crazy clothes and hair, she looked somehow dressed-up and very pretty anyway. "How are you, Pauline? I see you got out of jail alright."

"Well, not exactly alright." She raised her hand and touched her eye gingerly. "Benny wailed into all of us something fierce. I've got a load of concealer on my face, can you tell?"

Trinity, no stranger to makeup techniques, looked closely and admired the expert job that Pauline had produced.

"Benny did that?"

"Yes, ma'am."

"Can you tell the police?"

Pauline snorted, "That's not exactly the way it works, Miss Trinity. The problem now is that I ran away from him. I know he's after me, and if he catches me, he'll do a lot worse than this. Benny can be a gentleman sometimes, but mostly he's a lunatic."

Trinity gasped with horror, "Oh good Lord, Pauline! Have you got family you can get to somewhere?"

"No, I'm afraid not. They're all dead."

"Then, where can you go to get away? You've got to get out of here and away from all this!"

"Yes, ma'am. I know that I have to get out. I know the hell out of that! That's why I'm here."

"Here?"

"Yes, about that job," Pauline said, with very little hope in her eyes.

"You want to work here?"

"Yes, if you'll have me. You're the only person I know who is not in the business, or a cop. Truth is, Miss Trinity, I need your help. I need to get away from Benny, or one of these days, he's gonna kill me dead. I figure a nice lady like you could teach me some skills so I can stop working nights, you know?" she looked uncomfortable but determined.

Trinity was dumbfounded. She did not know what she could do for the woman. Looking around the gallery, she said slowly, "I'm not sure I have a job here for you, Pauline."

Pauline looked squarely into Trinity's eyes, "Miss Trinity, I'll sweep the floors, take out the garbage. If you need someone roughed up that didn't pay you, I'm your girl. I'm real strong, and I can move stuff around for you too." To demonstrate, she grabbed a large, rare piece of sculpture around its middle and started to drag it across the floor.

Trinity's eyes went wide, and she squeaked out, "Wait, Pauline! That's a very costly piece!"

Pauline backed away from the sculpture, apologizing, "Just showing you what I'm capable of,"

Trinity thought, *"There's no telling what she's capable of—that's what I'm afraid of."* But she looked at the hopeful woman in the blinding pink dress and saw a person who was in real need and willing to work for a better life. She read fear and hope, both, in Pauline's face, and she knew what she had to do.

"You'll need a place to stay, Pauline. Go get your things and bring them here. We'll get you situated in my place temporarily, and then I'm going to introduce you to some friends that might help."

"My suitcase is already right outside the door, Miss."

"You did say wine, right?"
—Dawn

CHAPTER 9

Dawn was talking to her best friend and Gumbeaux Sistah, Lola, on the phone that afternoon, saying, "It's taken months to get all of my affairs in order since the funeral. I'm just now coming up for air. Some of it took time, and some of what had to be done—like cleaning out his closets—I just didn't have the heart to do. Just arranging for Dan's funeral alone was almost too much for me, Lola."

"Give yourself a break, girl. You've been through the mill. No one is expecting you to have it all done instantly."

"Maybe so. It's been hard. And it also taught me that I'm going to have myself cremated. Funerals are too hard on people—the planning, the graveside. It's horrible. Cremation is easier."

"I've decided to be cremated too," said Lola.

Dawn started laughing as she said, "Oh, they wouldn't dare cremate you—not with all the wine you drink. The alcohol would blow the crematorium sky high!"

Lola chuckled, "Look who's talking. And I see you've still got your highly inappropriate sense of humor.'"

"Lola, honey, if I didn't, I would have been in the crazy house long ago." She changed the subject, "Speaking of making me crazy—I still don't know what I'm going to do with the thirty-thousand dollars Dan and I put aside to give to a local cause. I'm not sure I would have even remembered it existed. Dan took care of it, adding to it little by little. It's tough. There are so many causes to choose from. It's completely confusing. I wonder why he left it for me to decide and didn't just do it himself."

Lola shrugged and said, "It's strange, isn't it? He could have done that or at least discussed it with you before this. But if you really want my help, I can make some suggestions, if you'd like."

"Well, maybe. Give me a few days, and maybe I'll bring it up at the next Gumbeaux Sistahs meeting. Someone is bound to have an idea, don't you think?"

"Of course they will. Those women are full of ideas. Meanwhile, hang in there, girl. Thank God that your granddaughter Zoe is coming to visit you in a few days. I hate to think of you all alone over there going through this."

"I'm doing OK, Lola. I'm just crying *most* of the time now and not all of it," she chuckled. "And yeah, I haven't seen Zoe in a while, and she's always a pleasure."

"How old is Zoe now?"

"She's seventeen and one tough cookie, like her mom. But she is fair and has a good heart. And best of all, she makes me laugh. Zoe told her mother that she would stay with me for a few weeks to help out. What a sweetheart, right? I'm getting Zoe's room ready as we speak. The sistahs are meeting on Friday at the gallery, so I'll see you there."

"How about if I bring over some Crawfish Monica tonight, and we can have dinner together and crack open a bottle of wine?"

"Shoot, bring it over now! And you did say wine, right?"

"Do I know my best friend, or what?" laughed Lola.

Lola hung up the phone and turned to her husband, Bud, whom she had re-married only a few months ago. "Can you live without me tonight, Bud? I think Dawn could use a little company."

"Of course," he said, "How is she?"

"Hangin' in," said Lola with a sympathetic shrug, her red hair falling in soft natural curls around her face. "Our girl is tough, but this is a lot for anyone to deal with."

"Well, don't forget the wine," laughed Bud.

"Goes without saying," answered Lola with a wink. "And the sistahs are meeting Friday, thank God. I could really use their help."

"Help with what?" he asked, pouring himself more coffee. "Anything I can do?"

"Hmm, I'm not sure," she said doubtfully. "You know how I agreed to be on the board of the Safe House this year?"

"The domestic violence survivor's shelter, right?"

"Yep, that's the one. Well, as you know, I have a lot of experience locally with activism—you know how I'm always picketing for one cause or another around town. I've even done some picketing for the Safe House when their matching funds from the state were threatened."

"Somebody's got to do it," he said, giving her an affectionate kiss on her cheek. "I'm proud of all the difference you've made in our community."

"Thanks, sweetie, but this is a little different. I've supported the Safe House in the past, but now I'm in charge of all fundraising for the organization. I may have bitten off more than I can chew. The Safe House has its regular supporters, thank God, but they always need more money to make up for extras and the rising costs of care."

"So, what are you going to do?"

"Good question! I've been wracking my brain, but nothing is coming to me. If you think of something, let me know, OK?"

"OK," he nodded skeptically. "But this is not exactly my wheelhouse. I'm not a lawyer, activist, landscaper, plant sculptor like my beautiful wife." Bud owned a well-established nursery business—Broussard Nurseries. "True. I'm always good for a donation, but fundraising ideas? Yikes!"

Lola looked at her husband with a smile. She still could not get over how lucky she was to have married him—again. She and Bud had been married when they were very young. Too young. They divorced and went on to live separate lives. Bud had twin sons with his second wife, and Lola had joined the Peace Corps. Afterward, she opened her own landscaping business. Bud eventually divorced his second wife, and years later, he met up with Lola by accident in a local store. It took about two minutes for him to realize that a part of his heart had always remained with Lola. He asked her to re-marry him less than a year ago, and their surprise wedding had been the talk of the town. She remembered how handsome he had looked that day. He was always the lean and mean type, but he was also one of the kindest people Lola had ever met. Lola suddenly realized she had been daydreaming about their wedding for a second as she focused back on Bud talking again.

"Besides, you know that my days are tied up with warding off little-old-lady criminals in the nursery." He chuckled when he said this but rolled his eyes too.

"Oh no!" said Lola. "Is Mrs. Albertson at it again?"

"She never stopped, Lola. She still comes in at least once a week."

"She may be a little old lady, Bud, but she's still a crook."

"I know. I know. But what am I supposed to do? Throw a sweet old woman in the slammer for stealing cuttings from my nursery plants?"

"But it's not just one or two cuttings. She must have taken hundreds of them by now. And she never pays for anything. She's caused some damage to many of your plants as well."

"I know, it's a crazy problem to have, Lola. But it would be like throwing my mom in jail. I've got to come up with some solution to this, though. There's got to be a nicer way to stop her."

"You're such an old softy, Bud." She patted him on his shoulder. "And, of course, that's why I love you. That and because you're a hot, silver fox too, of course."

"That goes without saying, too," he winked.

Lola grinned, then she groaned, remembering her fund-raising problem. I'll bring the issue up to the sistahs on Friday. Maybe they can help."

"Are you sure we're related?"
—Dawn

CHAPTER 10

Dawn heard the doorbell ring, and her large frame came up off the kitchen barstool more quickly than would appear possible. She was a big woman but still supple. Before she opened the door, Dawn smoothed back her perfect brown hair and straightened her tunic top made of the expensive fabric she favored. She opened her front door wide and immediately scooped her granddaughter into her big, strong arms. "Zoe!" she screamed, then she held the girl with her reddish-blonde hair and smattering of freckles at arm's length. "Let me look at you! I haven't seen you in so long. You look absolutely gorgeous!"

Zoe Abadie grinned up at her grandma, her large blue eyes smiling, "Mamere! I'm so happy to see you!"

Dawn answered happily, "No more than I am. Thank you for coming."

"I'm happy to be here for you, and honestly, it's a good time for me to get away and be here too."

"How long can you stay? Till you're forty?" joked Dawn, and they both chuckled.

"I'll stay for a while, for sure." Zoe hoisted her petite frame onto Dawn's bar stool at the kitchen island. "How are you holding up, Mamere?"

Tears immediately sprung into Dawn's eyes, shocking even herself, as thoughts of Dan jumped to mind. Forcefully, she pushed them aside with a sigh, "Oh well, I'm a bit of a mess, but I'm doing

OK, I guess. Thank God for my friends, the Gumbeaux Sistahs. I can't wait for them to meet you. And Trinity is dying to see you too."

"Oh, I love Aunt Trinity. And if the Gumbeaux Sistahs are anything like you, then I'm sure I'll have loads of fun with them."

"Yeah, they are a hoot, and you'll see them soon. But right now, let me show you your room, and then let's get you some lunch."

"Mom warned me that you'd try to feed me a little too well."

"Oh well, your mom has a big mouth! But you can sue me later—like after lunch," she said laughing. "Might as well live a little, granddaughter!"

Zoe grinned, "I'm pretty sure I could get used to it."

When Dawn showed the young woman to her room, Zoe said, "I'm going to scoot out to the car and grab my suitcase."

"Need any help?" asked Dawn.

"No, not really. I'm a light packer."

"Really? Are you sure we're related?" joked Dawn.

The phone rang just then, and Dawn grabbed it, "Hello, Helen, what's new?" She listened a moment and then said, "Ooh, you are the best, sistah! Come on over." She hung up and said, "Zoe, go grab that suitcase and bring it in. That was Helen. I was going to make us some sandwiches, but Helen's coming over in a minute. She's picked a bunch of her tomatoes this morning and is coming over with her homemade tomato soup that she made especially for you. Her ward, Cooper, is coming too. He's about your age. This will be great. Helen makes amazing soup, and I don't know about you, but I'm starving!"

"Coming right up," said Zoe, heading out to the car.

She tugged her suitcase out of the truck and slammed the door closed. She stopped for a moment on the sidewalk and fingered the colorful luggage tag attached to the handle. It had an image of a huge tree with a tiny acorn underneath it with the caption *Dream Big*. Her father had presented it to her before she had left that very morning. He told her, "I'm so glad you're taking some time to go see your grandmother, Zoe. She needs us more than ever, and I can't possibly get away for more than a day right now. And I think you need some time to yourself to think. You still haven't explained to your mother and me why you are considering sitting out your first semester of college. I've tried and tried to talk to you, but you haven't been very forthcoming. Keep in mind that sometimes it helps just to talk about whatever is bothering you. I just hope that this little break away from us will allow you to figure out where your head is so you can come back and start school. The sooner you get your accounting degree, the sooner you can join the firm and have your own money and freedom. And believe me, that is a great feeling. Your mom and I would love to see your future secured. We worry sometimes."

Zoe shook the thoughts away and headed up her grandmother's sidewalk with her load—the suitcase and a heavy heart. Accounting may spell money but not necessarily freedom or love or anything else to Zoe. It seemed to spell imprisonment to her. But her family owned one of the largest accounting firms on the Northshore, and they were expecting her to join the firm. It had never even been in question. It was simply taken for granted that she would join and that she would be happy doing it.

Zoe loved her dad and her family and was deeply appreciative of all the firm had brought to them, but she was not convinced she wanted to work there. But when anyone asked what her plans were, she simply couldn't tell them because she didn't know herself. They assumed she would become an accountant by default. The problem had stumped her over the years—and then depressed her. So much so, that when Grandpa Dan had passed, she decided that she would visit Mamere, whom she had always admired for her living-out-loud attitude.

She needed a little living-out-loud herself right now.

“Be right there, Coop!”
—Helen

CHAPTER 11

Helen stood at the stove putting the final touches in the pot of her tomato soup. She strained on her tiptoes to reach the container of homemade croutons she kept on the top shelf. She was a petite woman, and the long, flowy, purple outfits she favored made her look more so. She brushed a strand of her brown, curly hair out of her eyes as she worked.

She had just phoned Dawn to say that she and Coop would be over in a minute to share the new batch for lunch. The Sistahs always teased her, saying that her soup was magic. They often called her Witch Hazel for fun, which tickled her. Of course, there was no actual magic in the soup, but there were so many fresh organic ingredients in it that it might as well have. It made a body feel incredibly healthy.

Helen had an intuitive hunch that told her she might be needed at Dawn's house today and that she had better bring Coop. She had long ago developed the habit of listening to her intuition and the Sistahs respected her hunches as well. They called it her magic. She realized that intuition might feel like magic because you cannot see it, touch it, smell it, taste it, or hear it. That is why it is sometimes referred to as the sixth sense. Carl Jung called it Collective Unconscious. Albert Einstein is known to have said, "The only real valuable thing is intuition." And self-help guru, Wayne Dyer, once said, "If prayer is talking to God, then intuition is God talking to you." Helen embraced that last theory wholeheartedly. She also believed that strengthening one's intuition requires exercise, like a muscle. She paid careful attention to her feelings that came up in her life—positive and negative feelings, both. She asked herself questions like, *Should I go on this trip?* or *Should I make this investment?* and then gave herself permission to take her time about making decisions. The answer always became clear after a while.

Lately, she had asked one particular question of her intuition. She was trying to have patience while waiting for the answer, but the waiting was hard this time because there was so much at stake. Coop was at stake.

As if on cue, Cooper walked in as she was stirring the pot, holding two of his latest paintings. During the past year, he had sprouted up on Helen's good food and care. He was still gangly but was over the six-foot mark now. His reddish-brown hair was growing in a bit darker, and his features were beginning to show the man he would be one day. He had taken up art this last year, and already Helen thought that his work was astonishing. It was full of dark contrasts, sharp angles, and raw feelings, from anger to frustration to rage. It made her think of a pot ready to boil over. He channeled all his emotions into his art. Helen had suggested that he bring them over to Dawn's at lunch today to get someone else's opinion. She didn't entirely trust her own because she thought everything the boy did was astonishing. He was so bright, so capable, and so loving in his dark, quiet way. The darkness was left over from his truly horrible past.

He and Helen found each other when he had come to do some tech work for her at one of her workshops. She hired him from his high school workforce office. It was a touch-and-go relationship at first until Helen found out what a horror his real life was at the time. His abusive stepfather had been forcing Coop to hide out away from home. He had a house but was virtually homeless, sometimes sleeping in people's garages and unlocked cars to get away from the drunkenness and the beatings. Getting enough food had always been a problem, too.

With the help of Social Services, Helen got custody in the courts as a foster parent, and she and Coop had been together since. Cooper now felt free to explore his life and talents, including art, instead of using them for mere survival. His temperament and temper were still well intact, but mostly it amused Helen now, and her amusement calmed him. Theirs was a complicated but genuinely loving relationship. Helen didn't know what she would do without the boy now.

"Hey, Miss Helen," he called to her from the next room, "Can you come here a second? I'm not sure which of these paintings to bring to Miss Dawn's place."

"Be right there, Coop," she called back, loving that he valued her opinion.

"If you don't pursue this talent, I'll hunt you down and paint you blue, understand?"

—Dawn

CHAPTER 12

Dawn opened the door for Helen and Cooper as they made their way inside with a pot of soup and the paintings.

"Hey Coop," said Dawn fondly and squeezed the young man in a reluctant bear hug. "Come meet my granddaughter, Zoe. You both have so much in common since you both just graduated from high school."

Zoe looked up cautiously from her seat on the kitchen bar stool. "Hey, Coop," she said quietly. She took in his black jacket, black t-shirt that said NO, and longish hair.

With his usually brooding fashion, Cooper nodded at the girl and merely said, "Hey." He took in her neat, white polo shirt, expensive Docker style shoes, and quality, beige slacks.

"Little entitled rich girl," were the words that zoomed across his mind.

"Wannabe outcast," were the words that zoomed across hers.

Helen and Dawn stood in the doorway and stared as if they were watching a movie. Helen hadn't even set down the pot of soup yet.

The two teenagers didn't say another word to each other, each sensing judgement from the other. So, Helen jumped in, "Coop brought a couple of his paintings over to show you, Dawn. I don't know much about this sort of thing, but I think he's got real promise here. I wanted him to show you and Judith. He's thinking of majoring in art."

"Let's see, Coop," said Dawn. "I love creative people, so you've come to the right place."

Cooper held up the two paintings side by side for Dawn to see. Zoe came and stood next to her to get a good look too.

Dawn didn't say anything for a minute. Then she turned to Helen, smiling, but addressed her comment to Cooper, "As your unofficial auntie, Coop, I'd say that these are uncommonly good. If you don't pursue this talent, I'll hunt you down and paint you blue, understand? And, as a businesswoman," she went on craftily, "Let me just say that I'll take these off your hands for a song so I can resell them in the gallery for a whole bunch of money."

Helen clapped her hands and went into a happy dance while Cooper looked on and smiled shyly. "Thanks, Aunt Dawn," he laughed. "If you're serious about selling them in the gallery—that would be awesome. Let me hold off there for a little while, though, and I'll paint more for you. I may need these as a work sample if I apply to art school."

"I'll be ready when you are," said Dawn. "Who knew you'd be adopting pure talent, Helen?"

At the word "adopt," the room grew quiet, and Helen and Cooper both looked uncomfortable. Helen broke the silence saying, "Well, Coop, let's pack these up. I still want you to show Judith. She might have some suggestions for you too."

Cooper quietly complied and carried the artwork out to the car.

"Did I say something wrong?" asked Dawn when he was gone.

"No, of course not," answered Helen. "But remember, Coop is not adopted. He still has that horrible stepfather who is in jail for abusing him. We're taking this very slowly. I get the feeling that Coop, while happy to be with me, is untrusting of family ties. I think he thinks that as long as he is just my ward of the court, it will keep enough distance between us to keep him safe. I don't blame him one bit, really. He's been through so much."

"Is that why he's so rude to people? So superior?" asked Zoe, surprising everyone.

Dawn gasped. Helen just stared at her with sadness. Then Helen said, "Uh oh. I hope nothing happened between you two. You know, he's come out of a terrifying, abusive background, Zoe. He tends to act superior to anyone who didn't come from his background. I think in his mind, he's accusing them of feeling superior to *him*. But he's brilliant, Zoe, and has a good heart, really. And he's getting better all the time. His 'aunties' and I are loving him to death, and we're feeding him the best food in town!"

"Speaking of which, let's dish up some soup for these kids," said Dawn. "I'm starving!"

"Wow. That is so rude!"
—Zoe

CHAPTER 13

While the two sistahs got the table set for lunch, Helen asked if Dawn needed any help around the house. She knew Dawn was still dealing with the aftermath of Dan's passing.

"Oh, I'm getting through it, slowly but surely. But there is one big bugaboo that's driving me crazy. I wish I could figure out what to do about the money in that charity fund that Dan left for me to allocate to a good cause. Shoot, there are so many causes to choose from, and thirty-thousand dollars can make a difference. "

Helen thought a minute then said, "Well, let's see—I guess I'd lean towards fighting a disease, or hurricane survivors, or saving the earth . . . oh good heavens! That is a tough choice, alright. Better bring it up at the Gumbeaux Sistahs meeting. Someone will have an idea."

"I hope so. It's driving me crazy. Who knew it was so hard to give money away!"

They ate Helen's delicious soup together, with Helen and Dawn chatting first with Zoe and then with Coop. However, the latter two didn't talk very much to each other. When lunch was over, Dawn got to her feet suddenly and said, "Helen, you've got to come see my vegetable garden. I know it's not up to your level of gardening skills, and never will be, but I've got summer squash started, and I've never grown it before. Come and see."

When they stepped out the back door, she whispered to Helen, "I just thought we'd give the kids a few minutes to themselves. They're both such independent and stubborn little monkeys. It reminds me of dogs I've had. They have to be taken out and socialized once in a while, or they get weird on you. Let's let these two socialize a moment."

Helen laughed. "It's a good idea. Coop needs exposure. He worries me sometimes. He needs young friends and doesn't seem to have any."

"Well, let's just you and I give them a few minutes. That way they won't suspect what we are really doing out here—stalling."

Back in the kitchen, Zoe took a sip from her water glass and said to Coop, "Well, my Mamere and your Aunt Helen apparently want us to talk to each other."

"Lucky us," said Cooper, rolling his eyes.

"Well, you don't have to look so happy about it," she said, disgusted. "You know they're forcing this on me too."

"Do what you want," said Coop, turning his attention to stare out the window.

Zoe glared at him incredulously.

He shrugged and glanced at her. "Besides, what would we even talk about?"

"That's a little more like it," thought Zoe and then suggested, "What about school? Where are you going to college?'

"I don't know yet. My grades weren't great, and money is pretty tight. I doubt if anyone would give me a scholarship, but I'm gonna apply and see what happens."

"Why aren't your grades good? I thought you were supposed to be some sort of genius," she blurted out, regretting her sarcastic tone instantly but unable to take it back at that point.

He flashed her a dangerous look. "Oh, I don't know," he said in a mocking voice. "Maybe it has something to do with being homeless half of last year. But what would you ever know about something like that? Your grandma's rich, and your mom and dad are probably rich too. Is that your car out front?"

"Yes, it is. So?"

"Yep. Did your mom and dad give you that? Of course, they did. You have no idea what it is to be real in this world."

"Wow. That is so rude! What do you know about me? Nothing, as it turns out. And I thought you were supposed to be smart."

"Where are you going to school?" he asked pointedly.

She flushed. "I got a scholarship to Tulane—majoring in Accounting."

"So, good grades, right?" he demanded.

"Yes, I did get the grades. What's your point?"

"A good, expensive school, a car from mom and dad, and a scholarship. Good grades are a lot easier to get when someone gives you the freedom and time to study. I'd say you've got it made, Miss Accountant."

That last part stung, and Zoe looked down and repeated the words softly to herself, "Miss Accountant."

"Yeah, that what I said. You'll be an accountant, and you'll be rolling in your parent's money all your life."

Zoe looked him in the eye, hurt in her voice, "That's just it, though. I don't know if I want to be an accountant. My parents are both accountants, and our family firm is doing very well, but it's just that . . ."

"You're kidding, right? The world hands you a free ride, and you don't take it? You're the worst kind of entitled there is."

"Look, I know you've got this whole thing going on of being a smart-ass jerk, but could you stay out of my face with it? I don't know what I want to do, and I came here to figure it out."

"Well, don't let me get in your way," he said.

"Can't see how that could possibly happen."

They were both fuming, and Dawn and Helen chose that moment to walk back into the kitchen as Coop, scowling, took one last potshot at Zoe, "Just a spoiled, little rich girl."

"Just a rude, stupid jerk!" she shouted and threw her paper cup full of water at him across the kitchen and hurried back to her room.

Dawn's eyes went wide, and Helen gasped. "Well, that went well," said Dawn, rolling her eyes.

**“I don’t think he likes me.
And the feeling is pretty much mutual.”
—Zoe**

CHAPTER 14

It was Helen's turn to bring the gumbo to the next Gumbeaux Sistahs meeting, which occurred whenever anyone was in the mood for it—which was often. The meetings were usually held at one of the sistahs' houses, but they decided to meet at the gallery today. Helen asked Cooper to help transport the gumbo pot and the rice. Bea was bringing fresh French bread, and Bitsy was supplying sweet tea. Dawn, as usual, brought a bottle of wine and her little bowl of potato salad since she was the only one who liked the sacrilegious combination of gumbo and potato salad. Since Dawn's sister, Trinity, would be joining the group today, and she liked it too, Dawn brought a little extra.

The sistahs helped themselves to the steaming, hot rice and gumbo and sat in the cafe part of the gallery. Lola put fresh bread and butter on the tables.

Dawn and Judith had envisioned not just a gallery but more of a community center. So, they served coffee and baked goods, provided mainly by Helen, and allowed the area to be used as a meeting room for small local groups.

Judith was preparing a big bowl of food for Cooper as he positioned his paintings so she could view them. She caught a glimpse of one of the paintings just as she tasted a spoonful herself. She stopped and almost choked, gaping at the artwork in surprise.

Dawn piped up, "Can you believe this, Judith? Who knew this boy of ours was keeping this kind of talent all to himself?"

Judith turned from the work to Cooper and said with her eyes wide, "Coop, these are so incredibly good. They're bold and colorful, yet thoughtful. We could sell a million of these. In fact, can we please?"

Dawn and Cooper looked at each other and grinned. "That's just what I said," said Dawn. "But he needs these for samples for school. He's promised to make more for us, right Coop?"

He smiled shyly and said, "Sure thing."

"But more importantly," Judith went on, "They're good, Coop. You're really good! You're already an artist, and you could have this life if you wanted it. It's hard and heartbreaking at times, but it's the best in so many ways. Of course, I'm biased, but so what? I'm still right." She chuckled.

Cooper nodded, "I've pretty much decided to go for it. I mean school-wise. I want to major in art if I can figure out a way to pay for it. I could just start painting and not go to school, but there is a lot I don't know, and I want to know what I don't know. You know?" They all laughed.

"My nephew is adorable," said Dawn hugging him.

"Seriously though, that sentiment is the kind of thing you hear from superstar artists. If you don't know basic things, you might end up limiting yourself, right?" asked Bea. "But you'll figure it out. Go apply to art school and see what kind of financial help you can get."

"To start, I'd like to take some business courses too. I don't want to be one of those artists who doesn't know how to sell or market their own work. Or how to look after their money. These are skills I'll definitely want."

"You're waaaay too smart by half," said Trinity. "And already ahead of the game. So many artists I know just want to paint and not take care of business. That's great if it's just a hobby, but if you want to make a living at it, you need to educate yourself. And I can tell you that many artists I know don't know the first thing about sales or managing their business and finances. And not to change the subject, but these would be wonderful in my New Orleans gallery, too. I'm calling dibs after the Gumbeaux Sistahs Gallery has their showing."

Cooper grinned, "You've got it,"

The group was quiet for a few moments as they dug into Helen's gumbo and rice.

"This is scrumptious, Helen," said Bea.

"As you know, it's my mom's recipe," she replied happily.

"Well, my mom's gumbo is better than your mom's gumbo," said Dawn, grinning.

"And my mom's gumbo would wipe the floor with your mom's gumbo." teased Lola loudly.

Zoe looked from one sistah to another, stricken, wondering what in the world was happening. They seemed to have all gone a little crazy.

Bea saw her face and hooted with laughter. "Don't mind us, Zoe. It's an old joke between the sistahs. We're all convinced that each of our mothers made the best gumbo, and it cracks us up to tell each other just that."

"Oh OK, I get it," smiled Zoe, then she said, "Well, in that case, I'll have to be on Mamere's team. My great-grandmother's gumbo beats the pants off your moms' gumbo any day!"

"Atta girl!" shouted Dawn.

Judith interrupted suddenly, "By the way, did you meet Coop, Zoe?" She pulled the young man from the corner by the gumbo to the center of the group.

"Oh yeah, we met," said Zoe, rolling her eyes and turning back to the gumbo.

"Sure did," said Cooper with the same amount of enthusiasm. He turned suddenly and started gathering up his paintings. "Well, gotta split. Thanks for the gumbo, everyone. I'll catch y'all later." He walked quickly out of the gallery.

Judith looked from the closing door to Helen, "What was that all about?"

Zoe responded stonily, "I don't think he likes me. And the feeling is pretty much mutual." She looked around at the stunned faces, "Sorry—just sayin'."

There was an awkward silence for a moment, and Bea broke it, "Well, let's let that sit for a while, OK? This group hasn't met in a while so let's get to it. I think we have a lot to talk about today, so everyone, try and keep it short."

At that, the sistahs recovered from Zoe's bombshell and perked up as Bea called them to order. She was their unofficial leader, as it came very naturally to her. She had always been in a position of authority or training in her former corporate life, and when it came to quietly telling others what to do, she just did it. It took a little getting used to at first for each of the sistahs, but they quickly realized that they appreciated someone taking charge, so they didn't have to do it.

"First of all, I'd like to check in with Dawn and Trinity. I've been thinking and praying for you both so much. Dawn, are you holding up OK, dear?"

"It's been pretty rough," said Dawn, shaking her head. "I can't tell you how rough."

As a widow herself, Bea said, "I know it is. It's so hard to make others realize how painful it is to go through this, right?"

"At least my daughters have stepped up to take over managing the office to keep things going, so I don't have to worry about that," said Dawn, wiping her eyes against the tears threatening to fall. "I honestly don't see how I could take care of everything there right now. I can barely manage to take care of myself. You know, it's impossible to tell others how it feels except to say that sometimes losing a spouse feels like you died a bit yourself. So basically, you don't feel like doing much because—what's the point if you're dead?"

"I know how you feel, dear. It's awful." Bea gave Dawn one of her huge hugs, and the rest of the sistahs crowded around her too.

Dawn shook her head, "And what's weird is that I feel it differently every day. Some days I feel anxious, confused, and afraid. Other days I just feel despair and even disbelief. It's such a hodgepodge of emotions. Sometimes, I even feel genuine pain in my limbs. And sometimes I'm just mad as hell. Mostly I feel like I just don't know which way to jump. I'd like to try to find a widow's group or something like that somewhere. But it sounds pretty depressing, doesn't it? I mean, I can't imagine going to a widow's coffee klatch. My imagination runs away with me about it. What do we serve—little muffins in tiny coffins? Funeral dirges playing in the background?"

Lola nearly spit out her coffee, "Well, you haven't lost your warped sense of humor anyway."

"Maybe digging up some widows' resources online might be better, I'm not sure."

Bitsy spoke up, "Well, I think you're doing really well, but that idea might be a good one. It's worth a try anyway. Leave the coffin muffins at home, though."

"She's right," said Bea, "You know, I heard from some women at church about a wonderful widow's website, www.widow180.com. I believe it has a podcast, blog, and many resources available through the site. A couple of the women were widows themselves, and they seem to think it's helpful. It might be worth checking it out."

"That's a good idea. Wait, let me write that down." She entered the website into the notes on her phone. "OK, thanks, Bea. Now, if I could only figure out what to do with all that money?"

"What money?" asked Bea, puzzled.

"I'll be happy to help you spend money for you," chimed in Trinity.

"It's not mine to spend. Well, not really." She told them about the thirty-thousand-dollar fund. "I'm supposed to give it to a worthy cause."

"That was so kind of both of you," said Bea, impressed.

"I'll admit that it was Dan's idea for the most part. He was a good man. I mean, it was my money too, but I let Dan manage the fund, and he kept up with it. But honestly, I just don't know which way to jump with this—any ideas, anyone? I've got so many choices, and believe me, I've thought of them all. Nothing seems quite right yet though."

"It's bound to come to you, Dawn," said Helen. "There's no hurry. Wait till the answer hits you. Then you'll feel better about your decision."

"You may be right, Helen. I've been in a real hurry to get it done, but I've also been worried I'll make the wrong decision, and making any decisions is a little tough during this time. Thank God I have Zoe with me for a while. It's great to have company in the house," Dawn smiled at her granddaughter who sat by the pastry counter again. Dawn had wanted her to come this morning to meet everyone, and so she could show her off as the brilliant, sweet granddaughter that she was.

Lola said, "Thanks for visiting, Zoe. I know your grandmother is a handful, but maybe she'll behave herself with you around." Dawn gave Lola a smart-aleck wink, and Zoe laughed appreciatively.

"What have you two been up to so far? Anything fun?" asked Lola.

"To tell you the truth," Dawn said quietly, "I feel a little bad. We haven't done much. I don't seem to be moving very quickly these days. I'm tired and sluggish, and well, just not the best company. Sorry, Zoe."

Lola jumped to her feet, saying, "It's understandable. You've been through the mill. You'll get back to being yourself again one of these days. Zoe understands that, don't you, Zoe?"

"Of course. I'm happy just to be here, Mamere," answered Zoe. "And to tell you the truth. I needed some quiet time myself to think about my future. So, it's all good."

Lola looked at Zoe, sensing conflict in the lovely, freckled, young face. An idea came to mind about how she could help Dawn entertain Zoe. "Zoe, I don't know if you like butterflies or not . . ."

"That's about the last thing I expected you to say, Lola," said Dawn, laughing.

"And who doesn't like butterflies?" chuckled Helen.

"Let me finish, please. I was about to say that I'm heading to the butterfly gardens out in Folsom tomorrow to see about doing some landscaping for them. If your grandmother can spare you, would you like to come with me?"

Zoe brightened, "Yes, I would. The weather here is great right now, and I could use a little outdoor adventure. Can you spare me tomorrow, Mamere?"

"Of course. Go and have some fun! I'll be just fine." Dawn shot a grateful look to her best friend.

"Great!" said Lola. "Helen is coming too. She wants to see if their gift shop would like to carry her essential oil line that she makes. It seems like a good fit for their store."

"Oh," said Zoe, suddenly crestfallen. "Does this mean Cooper will be there too?"

Helen sighed and answered, "No, he's got some things he's taking care of tomorrow. Something to do with applying to art school."

"Not a big fan of Coop?" asked Lola, pointedly with a glance at Helen.

"I think she made that pretty clear when she soaked him with water in my kitchen," laughed Dawn.

"It's more like he's not a fan of mine," grumbled Zoe.

The sistahs had already heard about the incident. Helen added, "Not to worry. He won't be there. Coop can be an acquired taste, but once you get to know him . . ."

Lola chimed in, "Maybe we'll just table the Coop issue for now. Helen and I will pick you up at nine tomorrow morning, Zoe."

"Great, I could use some butterfly time," said Zoe happily.

"I'm timeless! At least that's how I feel."
—Trinity

CHAPTER 15

"Moving on to other issues, sistahs," said Lola, finishing up her gumbo and changing the subject. "Trinity, you jailbird, I'm glad you were able to use your get-out-of-jail-free card. Have you seen the errors of your ways now, or are you just an old reprobate like your sister?"

Dawn sniffed, "Hey! Only the finest reprobates come from our family."

Trinity laughed. "Actually, Dawn's not kidding. We do have some crazy Cajuns in our family. Our dad's brother once took his riding lawnmower down I-10 for a beer run. Needless to say, Uncle Henry had already had his share of brewskies that day. Oh well, I guess every family has one like that."

Bea and Lola looked at each other and grinned. "OK, sure—if you say so." Lola teased.

"Anyway," Trinity went on. "I'm OK. I cleared it all up with the police thanks to Rocky coming to my rescue, and also to some of the girls I was arrested with—particularly the one named Pauline. She straightened the police out. They didn't want to believe that I wasn't part of their group at first, mostly because my hooker's costume looked more hooker-ish than any of the other girls did. I am good with costumes, as you know." She added the last part smugly.

"Oh boy," said Dawn, "I'm not sure it's appropriate to be bragging about your costume prowess in this situation. Anyway, don't you think it might have been your age that gave it away that the police made a mistake?"

"What age?" snapped Trinity. "I'm timeless! At least that's how I feel." She bristled at her sister, "Anyway, I just wish there was something I could do to repay Pauline. She's a nice girl; she really is. She's just stuck in a bad situation. She needs to get away from there. She's hooked up with what I suppose is her pimp—if they still call them that. And she's obviously terrified of him. I wish I could just pack her up and move her away from all that. Maybe get her a job somewhere. She needs a fresh start."

Nobody said anything for a few seconds, so Bea interjected, "Well, I think this will require a little more thought. Put your thinking caps on, sistahs. We'll circle back to this another time."

Judith suddenly asked, "How well do you know Pauline?"

"Not well, of course," answered Trinity. "But I know that she has a kind streak. She was trying to look out for the other girls and me throughout the whole ordeal. She is rough on the outside, but there's a hooker's heart of gold in there. I just know it."

"Well, I have no room at the inn," chuckled Judith, "My house is so crammed with stuff. But I could take her in for a little while if she doesn't mind the mess. And Dawn and I could give her a temporary job at the gallery cleaning up and maybe taking care of the pastry and coffee station. You know, just till we can find her someplace else. I feel like we need to help her. She obviously saw Trinity through a scary ordeal. Plus, if she comes across the lake, it might just be far enough away from her circumstances to make a difference. What do you think, Dawn?"

Dawn looked skeptical. "I'm not sure. Can we trust her? What do you think, Trin?"

"You know, when I dropped my cell phone, Pauline found it and returned it to me. She could have kept it and sold it. That says something about her honesty."

Judith said, "Well, maybe we could just try it for a couple of weeks until she finds another place. And we'll just be cautious about it."

Bitsy spoke up, "I might be able to get her some cleaning work down at the art museum as well. We're looking for someone part-time."

"OK, everyone give it some thought and see what you can do, and we'll talk about it in a day or two, OK?" asked Bea. "Now, who's next? Lola?"

"Hold the phone! I may have something for you."
—Judith

CHAPTER 16

"Yes," Lola said, getting to her feet. "Y'all know that I'm on the Safe House board this year."

"Oh no, are you over your head already?" teased Dawn.

"Absolutely not. Ok, yes I am," said Lola putting her hand to her forehead. "They want me to be in charge of fundraising. Apparently, the pickings must be pretty slim in that department if they asked me to take over. I have no experience at all at this sort of thing. Dawn, I know you and Dan regularly contributed to the Safe House, but if you want a suggestion from me, you can always donate that thirty-thousand dollars to them. Then all my worries would be over. If you're looking for a good cause, it's hard to beat the Safe House."

Dawn looked uncomfortable for a moment, then replied, "You know I believe strongly in the Safe House, Lola, but I'm not sure what to do with the money yet. I don't think you should count on it though because I feel like I'm missing something. I'm waiting for inspiration. I can't explain it well enough, but I know I'm supposed to do something specific with the money. I just don't know what it is yet. Sorry sistah, but please go ahead with your other plans for fundraising."

"What other plans?" asked Lola glumly.

"As you know, I've been on that board before," said Bea. "That fundraising position is a tough one. They always need a lot of help with it too. It takes a bunch of money to keep that place going. I'm sure they asked you because they know how creative you are."

"Creative or not, I'm desperate. Does anyone have any ideas for me?" howled Lola.

"You could do a black-tie gala," suggested Trinity. "Or a costume ball—I'd go to that!"

"We already have that kind of event scheduled for the fall. They do that every year. I need to come up with something extra to tide them over between events."

"Maybe give us a couple of days to think about this one, Lola?" suggested Helen.

"OK, but . . ." Lola started to say.

"Hold the phone!" shouted Judith, startling everyone. "I may have something for you!"

"Judith is on a roll this morning. What's on your mind?" asked Bitsy.

"I've been wracking my brains about what to do with all my old paintings that have taken over my whole house. But what if we did some sort of contest and I could donate those paintings as prizes? I'd need about a week of solid work to spruce them up a bit, make a few needed changes in some of them. But really, it's not too busy right now at the gallery, so I could take the time to do it. And truthfully, I just don't want them in my house anymore. I feel as if they are dragging me down. I hate living like that—like I'm some I'm sort of art hoarder."

"It's true. We'll have to send in a search and rescue to find her in there if she doesn't do something soon," said Dawn, grinning. "And if Pauline comes to stay with you, it will make it that much harder if you're all crowded into the house."

Judith was quiet for a moment, staring at Dawn. Then she blurted out, "Search and rescue! What a great idea!" Her eyes widened with excitement, and she paced the floor while she spoke, "Listen to this—we could hide the paintings all over town, like it was a huge, city-wide scavenger hunt! People could solve clues we give them to claim their prizes. I mean, I haven't worked all the details out in my mind yet, but give me a few days, and I'll come up with something—and I bet it would work!"

Lola jumped up with her mouth gaping, "Judith, you are a genius! I've never heard of this sort of event before. I think people would love it. We could whip up enough enthusiasm and get the whole town excited. The press could cover it, and I'll bet the mayor would include something about it in his city-wide emails. That would blow it up for us, and we'll get the radio, TV, and social media behind it."

"And the best part is that all the efforts will help some women and families. And my house will empty out and be livable again!" said Judith, smiling.

"This is an amazing idea. OK, let me present it to the board, and I'll get back to you. I'll bet they go crazy over it, Judith!"

"OK, I'll start working on the paintings to get everything ready."

"One thing," added Bea. "You'd better make a rule in your contest that only one prize can be claimed per person or family. Otherwise, you'll have one smart person ending up with a pretty good Judith Lafferty art collection, and the whole town will be annoyed at you."

"Good point, Bea. There are probably other considerations to make, but the basic idea is pure Judith-genius. Thank you, sistah! Let's get together soon to talk it all over," said Lola gratefully.

"Even I'm not that crazy."
—Dawn

CHAPTER 17

"Ok, anybody else have something to talk about?" asked Bea. She waited, then said, "Well, I have news, dears, but I'm afraid it's not good. I know you will all join me in saying some prayers when I tell you how sad it is."

"Is this about Lillian Deslattes?" asked Bitsy, who worked with Lillian at the Covington Art Museum. Bitsy was the director, and Lillian was chairwoman of the board.

"Yes, it sure is, dear."

"I can't believe it, can you? Tell them, Bea," said Bitsy, shaking her head.

"What happened?" asked Dawn. "I know this sounds awful, but I'm not sure how to feel about bad news and Lillian. That woman almost put us out of business when we first opened the gallery, and she caused Judith to lose her museum job, not that it didn't turn out to be the best thing that could have happened," she added, nodding at Judith.

"I know we've had some god-awful experiences dealing with Lillian in the past, dears, but this is different. She's in serious trouble."

"Tell us, Bea," said Lola, concerned.

"So, y'all know how I started hospital visitations this week through my lay ministry church program, right?"

"Yes, and we want to hear all about how that's going," said Helen.

"It's going beautifully, actually. There are so many people in trouble—I feel like I'm making a difference in a small but good way.

It's very fulfilling. But just guess who was one of the first people that I visited."

"Lillian? She's in the hospital?" asked Dawn.

"Yes, it was quite a shock—for both of us. She tried to throw me out of her room at first."

"Why is she there?" asked Helen.

"There was a terrible car accident near Slidell. She and her husband, Jack, were involved, and Lillian has a broken leg and wrist, some bruised ribs, a concussion, and what-all. She's a real mess, the poor thing."

"Oh my God," said Helen. "I wouldn't wish that on anyone! How is she? And how is Jack?"

"She's going to be alright, but she'll be in the hospital for a while, and recovery will take some time. She's really banged up."

"And the husband?"

"Actually, before she threw me out, she asked me to find out about him for her. She said they weren't telling her how he was."

"That doesn't sound good. Did you find out? Lillian has kids—they probably told her by now. If not."

"One of the nurses told me that Jack is not doing well. Not well at all. He suffered a bad head injury and he's in a coma. I'm going to see her again, and hopefully, the doctors have told her about Jack by now. If not, I just might. She has a right to know."

"It sounds awful!" said Judith. "As you know, Marty is Lillian's brother. He visited her yesterday and was just telling me about it. Those poor people."

"I was thinking about her all day yesterday," said Bea. "I think I should drop in again on her today. I want to make sure she knows what's happening with her husband and see how she's doing. There must be something I can do to help her. I was wondering if any of you would like to join me."

"Shoot, I would come, but it's my turn to stay here and keep the gallery open today," said Judith. The other sistahs also had important things to take care of—all except Dawn.

"I'll come," she said.

Lola laughed, "You're not going to kick her or poison her while you've got her at your mercy, are you, Dawn?"

"Even I'm not that crazy," huffed Dawn.

"I'm not entirely sure of that," added Trinity with a teasing smile.

"I'll stop by and pick you up at two. That poor woman needs our help."

"And no poison, Dawn," laughed Lola.

"She was brought up with a silver spoon sticking right out of her mouth!"
—Cooper

CHAPTER 18

When Cooper left the sistahs' meeting, he was disgusted over having to deal with Zoe yet again. *"What is her problem anyway? She's just a spoiled, little brat."* he grumbled to himself, then shook off thoughts of the girl as he made his way down the street. He didn't want her to ruin his day, which had started out well with the sistahs oohing and ahhing over his art. That meant an awful lot to him. He had grown fond of the sistahs and their unexpected zaniness, not to mention their enthusiastic acceptance of him being in their midst. They all claimed to be his "aunties." The idea made him smile. He had never experienced such joyful and sincere acceptance of his company and person. Not ever.

Since his mother's death when he was quite young, he had been left to live with his stepfather, Andre Dupre. Calling Andre any type of father was a misuse of the word. He was a drunk and a bully. Cooper had spent many years hiding from his beatings, often being forced into vacating the house at all hours to avoid them and being forced to sleep in neighbor's garages at night. He might as well have been homeless for half of his high school life. He had known hunger and loneliness, and because he kept things to himself, none of his classmates or teachers had known of his situation. He figured it would go on that way until he could graduate high school and manage somewhere on his own.

Then, Helen and the Gumbeaux Sistahs stepped in to help. Helen had pushed past his silence and discovered his living situation.

She took him into her home as a foster while a judge in Covington threw Andre in jail for child abuse. He had since been released, and word had it that he had started his life up again in Baton Rouge. Meeting Helen and getting away from Andre had been the greatest blessing of Cooper's life.

But old habits die hard, and Cooper still kept many of his feelings to himself. He was, at least, no longer rude and defiant to Helen and the sistahs as he had been when they first met. And while he was now fed, clothed, and had his own room with a bed to sleep in at Helen's house, a part of him still remained wary, suspicious, and in survival mode. Of deep concern to Helen was that whenever she brought up the subject of adopting him, his body language did one giant psychic flinch, and he changed the subject.

Allowing Helen that deep into his life would require a level of trust that Cooper had not known since his mother was alive. Trust had not been allowed into a life where guarding body and soul had been the norm for so many years. He did not even know what the word meant anymore. Letting Helen adopt him meant she would be in charge of him. He knew for a fact that only he knew how to take care of himself. He knew what it took and nobody else.

Of course, at this point, he believed that Helen was a sweet lady with good intentions. He felt she might even have some affection for him, and he sincerely appreciated that. But he thought, *"Shouldn't it take more than that to allow someone so deeply into your life?"*

No, it was better to control his own life and future.

He walked back home to look over the online applications to Loyola University, hoping but not really believing it was possible to get any sort of financial help that was available.

His thoughts turned once again to Zoe. *"And that girl!"* he thought about her, fuming. *"Why is she here anyway? She was brought up with a silver spoon sticking right out of her mouth. What a pain in the ass! I hope I don't have to see her anymore."*

Back at the gallery, Helen had watched Cooper walk out the door and was still thinking about him. Finally, she turned to the other sistahs, "I hope Coop is seriously considering adoption. He just won't talk to me about it."

"Give him time, dear. Coop has had so much to process this last year," said Bea, then added, "Adoption is not for everyone, though. Even if it doesn't work out that way, you'll still have helped him out during a very difficult period of his life."

"I know," said Helen, "but I'd really like to do more."

"When you get a chance to be this close to nature, it's a transformational experience."

—Lola

CHAPTER 19

Lola and Helen picked up Zoe early to make the trek to the butterfly farm in Folsom.

"I'm excited to see this place. I mean, who doesn't love butterflies?" asked Zoe, in high spirits.

"It's always a treat to go, and I'm happy to have a potential job there," replied Lola. "Helen is going to pitch her essential oil line to their gift shop manager while I meet with the owners. I did the original landscaping job at the farm, and now they want to expand it to the backlot. It should be a cool, little gig. I'm itching to get my hands on it."

Lola's excitement added to Zoe's, and she felt a surprising pang of envy. She thought, *"How lucky she is to have passion for her work. And Helen too. She obviously loves what she does as well. They both found their niches. Man, I sure wish I knew what mine is. I doubt seriously that it's accounting."* She inwardly groaned, *"Anything but accounting."*

"You're going to love this place. It's so beautiful," smiled Helen.

When they arrived at the butterfly farm, Helen went inside the cottage gift shop while the owners, Alex and Janet Miller, were waiting for Lola outside. Lola introduced Zoe as her assistant, and Zoe felt an odd sense of pride as she looked around at the charming property.

Lola's original landscaping had the property laid out with walkways lined with butterfly-friendly plants like alyssum, marigolds, petunias, bergamot, verbena, and many more. There were indeed quite a few monarchs making their way from one plant to another. But it wasn't until Lola pointed up into the trees that Zoe noticed the clusters, or roosts, of butterflies. Some of them were so large that they hung down and seemed almost to be dripping with the colorful insects.

Zoe gasped when she saw them, and Lola smiled knowingly, "Sometimes when you get a chance to be this close to nature and the outdoors, it's a transformational experience. It hits people in different ways. I can tell by your face that it didn't take you long to see it." She added quietly. "That's one of the things I love about this work."

Zoe grinned and said, "I get that. It feels so good to be out here. It's great just being around all the butterflies and plants and knowing that it was you who made all this so beautiful."

"Nature is beautiful all by itself," said Lola looking around happily, then laughed again. "But I give it a little nudge here and there to make the humans happy."

Janet Miller said to Zoe, "Lola does beautiful work. These butterflies were here before she came, but the grounds were a bit of a jungle. She turned it into a paradise for both the bugs and us."

"Turning landscapes into paradise—that should be your business motto," said Zoe.

"I'll remember that. Not bad!" Lola nodded appreciatively.

They walked back behind the cottage to the area where they wanted new landscaping. There was a large field with some old live oaks interspersed with tall cypress trees, their wooden knees sticking up out of the ground.

"This is a great space," said Lola, looking around, "What did you folks have in mind?"

"We're not sure," answered Alex Miller honestly. "We are counting on your magic, Lola." He had a big smile on his large friendly face.

"That's music to my ears. That way I can let loose with creativity," said Lola, grinning. "Hmm. Now that I've seen the property, let me take some photos and give it a little thought and get back to you in a few days."

"I have an idea!" blurted Zoe, then she flushed with embarrassment. She quickly looked at Lola and thought, *"Oh no, why did I say that? I have no business butting in here! It's just that I really do have an idea. It may be stupid, but who knows? I should have waited to tell Lola privately. What an idiot!"*

Lola looked her Zoe with some amusement, then said, "OK, assistant, let's hear it. I'm really curious."

Zoe, still blushing, pushed on, "It might be cool to build a butterfly-friendly maze back here. The butterflies would love it, and it would give people additional reasons to want to come to the farm. I mean, everyone loves a maze, don't they?"

Lola was quiet a moment and stood in thought. "You know, that's a pretty great idea. We could use the trees, the fencing, the vines and bushes, and planters to create a maze. I can picture a pretty stunning presentation."

Janet spoke up, "Can I just say right now that I absolutely love this idea. It's so much better than anything we could dream up."

Alex added, "And you know, we might just get a decent amount of extra income from it, too. People would come to walk the maze year-round, not just during butterfly season. It's kind of genius." He smiled at both Zoe and Lola.

Lola looked at Zoe, nodding, "And that, folks, is why she's my assistant."

Zoe flushed with pleasure.

On the way home, Zoe gushed, "Oh my goodness, Lola. I'm so sorry! I didn't mean to step over the line back there. That idea popped into my head and came straight out of my mouth! I usually have better boundaries than that, but I just got excited. It seemed like such a cool thing to do to that space, and I couldn't wait to tell you."

"Don't apologize. The client loved the idea, and it sealed the deal. And I loved it too." Lola smiled warmly at the young woman. "Actually, I think they might consider adding a sculpture garden to the maze as well. I have to run that by Janet and Alex, of course, but it could be beautiful, and I'll have a blast making it happen. I can envision it already. It'll be amazing when I'm done. Besides, it was refreshing to see you so enthusiastic about this work. It fired me up too."

"How did it go in the gift shop, Helen?" asked Lola.

"Great! They're going to start with a minimum order to see if my products are a fit for them, which they definitely will be. I think they'll do well with them, especially during the tourist season."

"Well, thanks to Zoe, we may just be expanding that season if we build the maze." Lola grinned. "Tourists may come year-round to walk the maze."

"That's good news," said Helen, smiling. She patted the young woman's arm, "Thanks for that, Zoe. That would boost my sales too."

"You're welcome," said Zoe, happily. She was delighted to have helped Helen out as well as Lola.

"Cooper and I will have to come back and see this maze when it's finished. I think he'd love that, and maybe it could inspire some new paintings," said Helen. At the mention of Cooper, Helen noticed that the happy look on Zoe's face faded into a scowl.

"Aw, Coop's not so bad, Zoe. He just takes a little getting used to. If I had lived the life he had, I would be a lot more than crabby. Truthfully, I'd probably be dead," said Helen sadly, shaking her head.

"What do you mean?" asked Zoe, shocked at Helen's words.

"Well, that boy has been through the mill. His mom died young, and his stepfather beat him every chance he got. He practically forced Coop to be homeless—and he was just a boy. But he's so smart that he scraped by. When he got a little older, he managed to get a dishwashing job and a few computer jobs through his school jobs department, including a job working for me. I had him create a slideshow for one of my workshops. But I'll admit—he was hard to take for a while."

"You should have seen him, Zoe," piped in Lola. "He was rude and arrogant, and he got in fights at school." She shook her head, then suddenly grinned, "But now we love him. And all the sistahs are his new aunties!"

Zoe looked stricken, "I had no idea."

"Yeah, it's true. But now he gets help from me and the sistahs. He lives with me in my home as a foster child right now. I'd love to adopt him, but this is where Coop still holds back. Every time I mention adoption, he freezes me out. I think it's still a trust issue—maybe it's kind of a powerful, self-preservation response. I know he's close to eighteen—when he can be on his own, aging him out of the foster care system—but I could still be his family and help him if he'd only let me."

"Give him time, Helen. It hasn't been that long, and he's been through so much," said Lola sympathetically.

"I didn't know," murmured Zoe, thinking about how she'd shut him down every time they talked.

"Well, how could you?" asked Helen.

"Speaking of knowing," interrupted Lola, thoughtfully, "Do you know what you are doing the day after tomorrow, Zoe? I've got a one-day landscaping job, and I could always use some help. Are you free? Would you like to be my assistant for a day? A real one this time?"

Zoe's face lit up with astonishment and joy, and she blurted out without even giving it a second thought, "Let's do it, boss!"

"You're looking at me like a starving man in a Burger King."
—Pauline

CHAPTER 20

That afternoon, Judith held the front door open and said, "Come on in, Pauline."

The woman with pink hair and a bright pink pantsuit with a bejeweled collar squeezed past Judith, holding a large, rolling suitcase.

"I can't believe I'm here, Miss Judith. Thank you so much for opening your home to me."

"I'm glad I could help you out while you figure things out, Pauline." She helped yank the butt-end of the large suitcase through the door. "Here, let me show you your room so we can put this right in there."

She walked down the hall while Pauline rolled her suitcase behind them.

"This is so nice, Miss Judith. It's very cozy."

"Please call me Judith. Are you hungry, Pauline? Would you like some lunch?"

"No, ma'am. I grabbed a burger and fries just before I got on the Causeway. To tell you the plain truth, I'm worn out. I've been so nervous, scared really, that Benny would find out that I was sneaking out. It's made me a wreck."

"I know you've been staying with Trinity for a few days now. Was it hard to get away and get to her place?"

"Not too bad. I have a roommate named Sheila, and she is Benny's new favorite. She would do anything for that lowlife. I'm embarrassed to say that I once felt the same way. At least I felt that way until I grew a brain. But you have to watch that Sheila. If she had suspected that I was moving out, Sheila would have had Benny on me like white on rice. And Benny doesn't talk with his mouth as much as he does with his fists, you know?"

Judith shook her head, horrified. "Pauline, you are doing the right thing. There's no need to spend your life with a monster like him." Then she added thoughtfully, "Maybe you'd like to take a nap for a couple of hours. I'll be in my studio in the back working. Just come and find me when you're ready and we'll have tea together. That sound alright?"

"It couldn't sound any better, Miss Judith," said Pauline, relieved.

"It's just Judith," Judith reminded her.

"Yes, ma'am," said Pauline, sitting down on the corner of the bed, already feeling the stress leave her body. Sleep would be right around the corner.

Judith left and closed the door behind her, and Pauline stretched out on the bed, placing her exhausted head on Judith's soft pillows and waited for sleep.

But the minute she closed her eyes, her brain began churning. She thought about Benny and the other girls and tried to remember how in the world she had gotten her life into the mess it was in the first place.

Her start in life had already been a bit of a mess. She was born and raised outside the small town of Gonzales, Louisiana. She and her four brothers and sisters were brought up in a two-bedroom, rundown house in the country. They were as poor as a sharecropping family could be, but she still felt lucky to have her family. She felt especially lucky to have her mother, who raised her with humor—always laughing and joking. Her father was the serious one. Pauline and her siblings went to school barefoot most days to save her good shoes from wearing out. She did well in school until she was fifteen years old when she met twenty-four-year-old Cedric "Tree" Treesom at the town carnival. Afterward, he started giving her rides home from school. Pauline liked being seen with Tree. It made her feel grown-up and cool in front of her school friends. When Pauline got pregnant, Tree offered to marry her, and it was a good thing because her father said she had to leave home so she wouldn't shame their family. He was ashamed of her, and that felt worse than the prospect of being homeless or marrying Cedric Treesom. She and Tree did get married when she was four months along, and they moved to an apartment over the tire store. At six months, Pauline lost the baby. She also lost any decent treatment or respect Tree might have had for her because of her condition. He worked at a car mechanic business in town, and on his way home, he would often stop for a few beers with his friends from the car garage. A couple of hours later, he would stumble home and, if his dinner wasn't to his liking, Pauline had better be able to outrun him. He caught her many times, and Pauline walked around with bruises all over for a few months. She put up with it until one night he passed out, and she carefully rifled through his pockets and took what money was left over after all the beers.

She had kept a small suitcase packed for just that moment, and she fled the house to the bus station where she stayed up all night watching out for Tree's appearance. He never showed, though, probably sleeping off his drink later than usual since she wasn't there to wake him for work. She caught the early bus straight to New Orleans.

She headed down to the French quarter where she took up with a group of young people who crashed in an abandoned house on Esplanade Avenue, often doing drugs. Pauline didn't know the names of the drugs, much less had any desire to partake of them. She smoked weed with the group, a lot of weed, actually, but she watched how, one by one, the young people slowly ruined themselves with harder drugs. Some of them even died. She was the only one with healthy skin, good teeth, and clear eyes.

She kept looking for work and finally landed a job working as a cocktail waitress at a Bourbon Street club. The money was not good, but she was determined to get out from living with the druggies and to get a place of her own.

After she had worked there for a few months, a man came in one night when Pauline was taking a turn working behind the bar. He took a stool and stared at her as she served beer and cocktails to one customer after another. He had ordered a beer for himself and made his way slowly through his drink, still watching her closely.

At some point, Pauline stopped in front of him and said bluntly, but with a smile, "You're looking at me like a starving man in a Burger King."

That got a slow smile out of him, and he said in a drawling, deep voice, "You're about the prettiest woman I seen in a long time."

Pauline, who was used to men hitting on her in the bar by now, simply said, "Thank you." She liked the way the man looked, his eyes were dark and hungry, and his smile flashed brilliant, white teeth. She liked his clothes too. He wore a suit that looked kind of expensive, like he was some sort of businessman, which is exactly what he said he was—in businesses of many kinds, and he would explain it to her someday when he got to know her better. That night she asked him, "So what's your name?"

"It's Benjamin Williams. You can call me Benny. And what should I call you?"

A glint of mischief sparked in Pauline's eyes as she said, "You can call me to come out with you for dinner, Benny. My name's Pauline."

He took a beat and looked her in the eyes. "What time do you get off, Pauline."

"My shift is over at eleven."

"Then, at eleven, I'll be waiting for you right out front."

And that was that. Benny took her out, wined and dined her, flattered her, and told her she was his favorite girl. It didn't take any time at all before she had moved out of the druggies' place and into

Benny's spacious apartment on St. Louis Street. She liked being called his favorite girl and believed she knew what he meant by that until she found out that Benny managed sex workers. Quite a few of them. They were his girls. In short, Benny was a pimp. She found out in the worst way possible.

When they first moved in together, he would say things to her like, "Why are you working your brains out at that bar, baby? You could be making so much more money—a pretty little thing like you. And it would be easy money." She thought that he meant she should become some sort of model, but she didn't believe that she was sophisticated enough for that. She told him that nobody would hire her to be a model.

He said, "I'll hire you to model."

"Whatchu mean," she asked, perplexed. "What kind of model would a businessman need?"

He told her that he knew businessmen who came to town occasionally for special events, and one of those events was coming up soon. He said he had hired several other models for the event, and she could be one of them.

"And," he added, "It pays five hundred dollars."

Pauline's eyes grew wide. Five hundred dollars was a lot of money to her, and she needed to get to the dentist. She'd had a toothache for the longest time, and the pain was getting worse. It only took her a second to say, "If you're serious, then I'll do it. Thanks, Benny," She thought, *"How hard could modeling be?"*

The night of the event, Benny drove her to a building in the warehouse district. There was no business name on the building, but it was a sound, brick establishment and looked decent enough to Pauline. She wore a pretty, short sequined dress that Benny had bought for her, and she did up her hair and makeup with extra care that night.

"What am I supposed to do, Benny? Is there a runway?"

Benny chuckled and patted her leg, "No, no. It's not that kind of gig. It's more of a hostess kind of thing. Kind of like you do at the bar—so it will be a breeze for you. You just walk around looking beautiful and serving cocktails to the gentlemen who come here to play cards."

"Cards?" asked Pauline, surprised. "I never heard of such a job." She wished she had known. She wouldn't have worn her high heels. Her feet would be hurting at the end of the night.

"It's easy money, believe me."

He escorted her inside and brought her to the kitchen area, where three other attractive women were loading trays with cocktails.

"This here is Pauline," he told them. "Tell her what to do." He turned to her and said, "Those gentlemen are waiting for me. This is a significant business event for me, Pauline. So just do what these girls do, and you'll be fine. And you'll get your money at the end of the night."

Benny was right; it was easy work at first. For the first two hours, everything went well, except that she found the other women to be surprisingly hostile to her. They ignored her and grunted commands at her when a table needed service. The men, however, were playful with her, bordering on being a little handsy, but Pauline knew how to dodge that nonsense.

At midnight, she saw Benny signal to one of the other women, who then grabbed Pauline by the arm and hurried her back to the kitchen, saying, "C'mon. Move your ass. It's time!"

"Time for what . . ." she started to ask but stopped and stared as soon as pushed through the kitchen doors. The woman who was hurrying Pauline stopped and started peeling off her dress right in front of her. Pauline looked around and found the other two women undressing as well. They got down to their panties only and high heels.

Pauline was speechless until she suddenly found Benny at her side. "What is this, Benny?"

He acted the innocent, "What do you mean, Pauline? This is the job. You didn't think it paid five hundred dollars just to look pretty, did you?" He saw how dismayed she was but ignored it. "Look, it's not a big deal. All you have to do is keep serving the drinks like you did before—just with a little less clothes on this time." He chuckled but smiled encouragingly. "Shoot, if someone paid me five hundred dollars, I'd serve drinks topless wearing a tutu, too."

One of the girls called over to Pauline, "Look, it's easy, girl. You don't have to sleep with them. Just look pretty. If they want to sleep with you, they will pay you a lot more." She laughed loudly, and the other women were nodding.

Pauline looked helplessly at Benny, and he whispered to her, "You can do this, Pauline. You're my favorite girl."

That was the moment that she understood it all. That was the moment. Even though Pauline had been disowned, married, beaten, forced to live with druggies in an abandoned house, it took Benny's betrayal to cause Pauline's innocence to leave her life. She no longer believed. She understood how complex the world was, and she had a decision to make. She needed money. She had to get to a dentist, and if she turned this gig down, she knew she would probably have to move out of Benny's place. But she knew she couldn't live on what they paid her at the bar. She needed Benny. She was stuck. She thought desperately, *"Maybe it won't be too bad, and then I'll have a little bit of money. Maybe I can make a new start somewhere down the road."* Her decision was made.

She slowly pulled her dress over her head and unhooked her bra.

"That's my girl, said Benny, smiling at her. "Go out there and make me proud. You look beautiful, better than all these other whores put together."

"Other whores," thought Pauline.

So, despite her qualms, Pauline bared her breasts for the next couple of hours and served drinks to drunken men playing cards. There were some sloppy moments dealing with the drunks, and then there were the hands that were all over her as she worked the room. But she steeled herself and told herself that it was just this one time.

But after that first night and that chunk of money, one time turned into two and then many more. It was a very short leap from just walking around topless to lying naked underneath strangers—at first with Benny watching murmuring encouragement, then later by herself.

Years went by, and Pauline discovered two things. One, when Benny didn't get his way, he did not hesitate to use his fists on his girls. She had suffered many black eyes and bruises and once even a cracked rib where he had punched her. And two, Benny had many "favorite girls." She was only one of them, and after a few years, she wasn't even that. She was just one of his girls. For many years, she wanted out, but as each year went by, the less she believed herself capable of doing anything other than working the streets.

So, when Trinity, Pauline, and the other women were arrested, Pauline took her for just another girl on the street. When Trinity turned out to be something else, it lit a fire in her heart. It inspired her to find out if it was too late for her. Trinity was her sign—her inspiration. She believed Trinity would hold her fate. So, she stepped up and took a chance.

"Shopping my eye! More like shop-lifting!"
—Doris

CHAPTER 21

Lola's husband, Bud, stood behind a large leaf palm and spied on the white-haired, old lady who was strolling casually down the next aisle in his nursery. The woman, whose name was Mrs. Albertson, stopped every so often, looked around surreptitiously, and then took out a pair of silver sewing scissors. She snipped off a small plant cutting, her fifth in as many minutes. Bud had seen her cutting each one and carefully placing it in a plastic bag with what looked like a wet paper towel inside. She then returned the plastic bag to her large purple tote bag.

This was not the first time Bud had caught her making cuttings of his nursery stock. He had complained to Lola several times that he didn't know what to do about it. Most of the time, it was not that noticeable, but there were a few times when she would take a cutting from a more valuable plant or even a plant that was too small to support a cutting. It had damaged several plants. Bud was beginning to think of her as an ancient locust descending upon his crops. The trouble was, he didn't know what to do about it. She was such a sweet-faced lady and always so polite and happy when he greeted her in the store. He could not bring himself to fuss at her, or worse—have her arrested. Bud closed his eyes and shuddered to think how it would feel to see Mrs. Albertson having her head ducked down getting in the back of a police car. As he had told Lola, it would be like throwing his own mother in the slammer.

He thought about taking the coward's way out and asking Margaret, his assistant in the front office, to approach the women, but he knew that would be a mistake. Margaret was tough and no-nonsense. It could go badly very quickly. If Margaret made the old woman cry, Bud would feel awful.

He had made a half-hearted attempt earlier. "Good morning, Mrs. Albertson," he had said. "Uh, is there something you'd like to tell me?"

"Yes, young man, there is," said the sweet-looking woman with a smile. "You sure have a wonderful nursery here. I like so many of the plants. And you sure are a big hunk of a handsome man!" The old woman giggled.

He thought hopelessly, *"What am I supposed to say to that?"* He knew that Mrs. Albertson came to his nursery at least once a week, sometimes twice, and was driven and dropped off by another woman, maybe in her fifties, who drove a white pickup truck. He went to the front parking lot and sure enough, the woman was waiting in her truck for Mrs. Albertson, as usual.

Reluctantly, Bud approached the pickup. The side window was open, and he hesitantly cleared his throat as he walked up so as not to startle the woman behind the wheel.

"Uh, hello there," he said in a friendly voice.

The woman, who was listening to a podcast on her phone, startled anyway, "Oh goodness! I didn't see you!"

"Good morning," he said, "Sorry I scared you. I'm Bud Broussard, the owner of this nursery. I had to come over and ask you something."

"I'm Doris Buckley. I'm here with my mother, Vera Albertson. You've probably seen her inside. She loves coming here. In fact, she's mentioned you to me too. She thinks you look like John Wayne," she said, laughing.

Bud cleared his throat and sighed, "Yes, well, that's what I need to talk to you about. You see, we have a little problem with your mom. She seems like the sweetest thing in the world, but, well, you see, she's stealing from the nursery. And has been for some time now." He shuffled his feet uncomfortably and felt like he was tattling in school. "I hate to have to tell you like this."

The woman gasped, "Stealing? Mom?"

"Yeah, I'm afraid so. As you know, she comes once or twice a week, and while she's here, she takes clippings from many plants and then sneaks them out in her purple purse."

The woman looked horrified. "Oh no! I'm so sorry. I can't believe this. No wonder she always insists on going in by herself and leaving me to wait out here. She's so sneaky! She lives alone, you know? Doesn't drive anymore. So, twice a week, I take her to the grocery and to run errands. She always likes to stop here on the way home. She lives right up the street." The woman put her hand to her forehead, "Shoot, she enjoys coming here so much. She loves plants, and she has an amazing collection at home . . . Oh my goodness! What am I saying?"

"I'll bet she does," laughed Bud.

"Mr. Broussard, I'll be happy to pay for any damages she's caused."

"That's OK," said Bud. "But, of course, I've got to ask you to either not bring her here anymore, or maybe just accompany her when you do. I'd be OK with that. I hate to spoil all her fun—sounds like she's pretty lonely." He looked up suddenly and said, "Oh boy, here comes your mom now."

Mrs. Albertson ambled across the parking lot. When she saw that Bud was talking to her daughter, she hugged her purple tote bag tightly to her chest.

"Mrs. Albertson . . ." Bud began.

But the daughter interrupted loudly, "Mom! What have you been doing?"

"Shopping, of course," snapped the old woman.

"Shopping my eye!" said Doris. "More like shop-lifting!"

"Doris, you watch your tongue," she said sharply. Then she turned to Dan and said sweetly, "Before you say anything, young man. I just want to invite you over—wait, are you married? I sure hope not."

"Mom!" said Doris.

"Yes, ma'am. I sure am. Very married," answered Bud.

"Well, what can you do? Still, you're invited to lunch this Saturday. Bring your wife. I'll cook you something wonderful."

"But . . ." started Bud.

"No buts. Saturday at noon. Doris, you come too," she said, climbing in the cab, "Three-Seventeen Bonnabel Street—right up the street. Blue house. Let's go, Doris."

Doris looked from her mother to Dan and shrugged. As she started the car, she said, "Try to come if you can, Mr. Broussard. She's a great cook, but I'm her only company these days. It would mean a lot, and we'll work everything out regarding her little problem at that time, OK? I'd better go. There's no arguing with my mom." She rolled her eyes and took off.

Bud stood gaping at the retreating vehicle. Then he shrugged and pulled out his phone. When Lola answered, he said, "Honey, what are we doing Saturday at noon?"

"Marty is good at a lot of things."
—Brenda

CHAPTER 22

Judith was expecting Lola to drop by the next morning, but she had to run to Marty's beforehand. He needed to borrow a tablecloth for a display for his upcoming show. She rang his bell early, but no one answered, so she headed around back to his workshop. She walked up to the doorway and was just about to call out, but she was struck silent for a moment and her heart gave a lurch. Inside the workshop, she spied Marty standing very close to Brenda with his hands touching her face. They were looking into each other's eyes.

"Marty!" yelped Judith.

"Oh hi, honey. I'll be with you in a minute," Marty said calmly. It was that very calmness that confused Judith and prevented her from running away—or committing mayhem, one of the two.

Marty index finger darted into Brenda's open eye, and he said triumphantly, "Got it!" He opened his fingers for Brenda to see.

He added over his shoulder to Judith "Brenda had a pesky eyelash loose and couldn't manage to get it out."

Judith looked from Marty to Brenda and was shocked to see that the younger woman's expression was both openly hostile and victorious towards Judith. Brenda smiled smugly.

Judith nodded slowly, taking it all in. "And so, naturally, you volunteered."

"Well sure, and for future reference, it so happens that I'm good at it," said Marty, chuckling.

Brenda added, "Marty is good at a lot of things." Then she coolly sashayed by Judith on her way out. She called over her shoulder, "Thank you, Marty dear."

Marty came to Judith's side and kissed her cheek, "Oh, you remembered the tablecloth. Wonderful, and just in time!"

But Judith couldn't help but think that she might be just a little too late.

"Whenever I need extra cash, I just work the streets an extra-long night."
—Pauline

CHAPTER 23

Lola knocked on Judith's front door, and it was immediately opened by a woman Lola didn't know. The woman was in her forties and had on the shortest shorts in the brightest pink color Lola had ever seen. And they matched her hair.

"Hey there," the woman said. "You gotta be Miss Lola, the plant lady. Come on in."

Just then, Judith came in from the kitchen, wiping her hands, "Good morning, Lola, have you met Pauline?"

"Not officially. It's nice to meet you, Pauline."

Pauline walked straight up to Lola, holding out her hand. She grabbed Lola's hand in hers and shook it aggressively. "It's really good to meet you, too," she said with a large, toothy grin.

Startled, Lola laughed for a second then asked, "So, how are getting along here, Pauline?"

"Oh, never better! Miss Judith may be the best person in the whole world," enthused Pauline.

Judith sighed and said to Lola, "Lola, want some coffee? Go and help yourself in the kitchen. I just made some."

"You bet." Lola headed down the hall, and Judith turned and whispered to Pauline, "Tone it down a little, Pauline. You're coming off a little . . . I don't know. . . manic?"

"I'm not sure what that means but sure, I'm just anxious to fit in. Miss Trinity told me to try and do that. I'm just not used to normal people yet."

Judith giggled, "My friends are hardly what I'd call normal, but don't scare them off either. I need my friends!"

"Sorry, Miss Judith. I'll do better."

"C'mon, let's go have coffee."

They joined Lola in the kitchen, and she immediately jumped into the reason for her visit. "I have to admit, I'm so excited to hear more about the idea you had for the fundraiser."

"Fundraiser?" Pauline chimed in. "You need money, Miss Lola? You don't look like you need money, but OK, if you say so. Whenever I need extra cash, I just work the streets an extra-long night."

At that, Lola just lost it. She burst out laughing so hard she almost choked. Judith just stared at Pauline, momentarily dumbfounded.

Between bursts of laughter, Lola couldn't resist saying, "Pauline, between the two of us, Judith and I couldn't raise fifty cents that way."

"Hmph," laughed Judith. "Speak for yourself."

"With my help, and a little makeup, I could get your street value way up," said Pauline seriously.

Judith put a stop to that line of thinking, "Pauline, your 'street value' days are over. That's why you're here, remember?"

"Of course, I remember. I was just yanking your chain, Miss Judith." She gave Judith a tentative grin that convinced Judith otherwise.

"Please just call me Judith," she reminded her for the twentieth time.

"And just call me Lola, OK?"

"We're going to find you another way to make a living, Pauline. That's a promise from the Gumbeaux Sistahs."

"I'm grateful, really. And you know what, I'll help with your fundraising in any way I can."

"Yes, let's get back to that," suggested Lola. "I'm so excited about the whole idea."

"Good thinking. Ok, well, let me ask you something. What did you notice on your way down the hall to the kitchen just now?"

Lola thought for a second, then just walked to the door and peeked down the hall.

"Wait, I know," said Pauline. "It's the yellow paint on the walls." She turned to Lola, "Miss Judith just loves her some yellow paint! It's all over the house—inside and out! Now I love yellow alright, but sometimes this hurts my eyes to see it everywhere." She lifted her hand to her face and rubbed her shut eyes. "Maybe think about getting some pink in here someday," she added.

Judith looked at Lola, who was doing her best not to burst out laughing again. "No," said Judith through closed eyes. "That's not it." She added disgustedly, "Try again."

Lola took another peek down the hall and said, "The only things out of the ordinary are your wonderful paintings that line the walls. It must be hard to find space to store them all."

"Bingo," said Judith, giving Pauline one last sharp look. "I used to keep them in a rented storage unit, thinking that someday I'd get around to working on them. But that just puts them 'out of sight, out of mind.' And I've been paying storage fees on them for years. It's ridiculous. So, I dragged them back home again. But as you can see, they are everywhere. It's time to do something with them. So, I think, if we can pull it off, my treasure hunt idea might be good for everyone."

"I don't know all the logistics, but I can't wait to hear more," said Lola.

"Treasure? Oh, hell yeah. I'm in," said Pauline loudly, her eyes wide.

Lola guffawed, "So, let's go over it all again—how would it work?"

"OK, here's what I'm thinking. We could gather business sponsors, and every sponsor would pay some sort of sponsor fee to be able to host a treasure venue. All the sponsors would get a painting to hold for the treasure hunt. I have around twenty-five paintings, so we'd need that many sponsors. Then we would sell tickets to the hunt. A ticket buys you clues to the sponsors' locations which we will announce early in the morning on the day of the hunt. The ticket holders have till six P.M. that day to figure out the clues and head to a sponsor holding a painting. The clues will be all about the sponsor. For example, if Mo's Art Supply is a host, the clues might be 'Curly, Larry, and *blank,'* or 'Less is *blank*' Things like that. The first person to go to that painting's host can claim it. If more than one person arrives at the same time at a sponsor's we could declare a tie. Then a tie would require a coin flip. The winner would get the painting and the loser of the flip would get a print instead of the original painting. I've got some prints around here that I can donate too. Then that evening, the winners will be announced. If no one claims a painting, then it will be auctioned off at the end of the hunt. So, you make money from ticket sales, sponsor fees, and raffles. What do you think?" Judith held her breath, waiting for Lola's reaction.

"Holy cow!" said Lola, her mouth going wide in a grin. "I love-love-love it, Judith. You're a genius! No one else has done this, and people love your art, so it would be a huge draw. But what do you get out of this? What about all those paintings? Can't you sell them in the gallery?"

"Yes and no," answered Judith. "Here's what's true. They've been sitting around so long that I'm sick of them. They are clogging up my house and stealing my peace of mind. I just can't seem to get them ready to go for the gallery. But if I just took off maybe a week, I could whip through these, working on all of them at once and polish them up for the treasure hunt. Bring them up to snuff. Of course, I'd expect a whole lot of free advertising for the gallery in return. Plus, I still get to write off the paintings from my taxes. In some ways, you'll be doing me a favor. I'll get my house back!"

"It sounds like a lot of fun," said Pauline.

"It sure does," said Lola. "And that's what makes it so different. I can't wait to tell the Safe House board about it now that we have more details. Of course, they will have to approve, but why wouldn't they? It's a stroke of genius. And now that I'm thinking about it, we might do an event at the end of the treasure hunt. We can present all the winners with their prizes that night and raffle off any leftover paintings. It would be another source of income tied into the whole idea."

"I'll help," said Pauline excitedly. "Give me a brush, and I'll start spiffing up these paintings. Where's the pink paint?"

"You can help deliver the paintings, Pauline, and, well, there's going to be a lot to do. We'd better round up the sistahs and a host of volunteers to help."

"I'm sure all the sistahs will want to get in on this act. And Dawn is just going to love the free publicity we'll get for the gallery," said Lola.

"You bet she will. So will I," grinned Judith.

“Ok, when in doubt, the little black dress it is!”
—Judith

CHAPTER 24

Judith stood in front of her closet, trying to figure out what to wear that night. Marty had invited her out to dinner and told her they were heading to Del Porto. She was excited not only because she loved the Italian food at that restaurant but also because Marty had taken her there for their first date.

She thumbed through the hangers and finally said out loud, "OK, when in doubt, the little black dress it is." She added a royal blue shawl and silver earrings to complete her look. She had to choose between a pair of sparkly, silver shoes or a more comfortable, sensible black heel. She chose the sensible pair, thinking that no one would notice.

At last, she was ready, and Marty picked up her a few minutes before their seven o'clock reservation. The restaurant was only a few blocks away. When she opened the front door, he whistled appreciatively and said, "I am one lucky so-and-so, Judith Lafferty."

"Yes, you are, Marty LeBlanc." She looked admiringly at his dark blue suit and tie—but mostly his handsome face. "That makes two of us. You look wonderful tonight. It's nice for me to get out of my painting clothes for a change, and I'll bet you feel like a million bucks in that suit."

"Well, shall we go?" he asked, offering his arm.

On the short drive over, Marty was noticeably quieter than usual. He seemed on edge about something.

"What are you thinking about? Is everything alright?" she asked him. He was a calm, reliable type of man. She was not used to seeing him wound up.

"Oh sure, sure," he said and laughed. "I'm just thinking about my upcoming show in Lafayette. I've got a lot of furniture to finish. It's weird having deadlines again," he said ruefully. He had been retired for a few years at this point.

"I'm sure you'll do fine. You always do. Is Brenda helping you out any?" she asked with a not-so-tiny wish that Brenda was not the all-freakin'-perfect assistant she seemed to be. There didn't seem to be anything the woman could not do. Judith was grateful to her for the help she gave Marty, but—and she was ashamed to admit this—she wanted to slap her too, especially for her flirtatious manner towards Marty.

"Yes, she is—that Brenda's the best," said Marty enthusiastically, making a slight scowl appear on Judith's forehead. He went on, "Don't mind me. I'm just a bit on edge about it all, but it will pass after one glass of champagne, I'm sure."

"We're having champagne?" asked Judith jokingly. "Wow, you do love me!"

"Matter of fact, I do," he said and reached over and placed his warm hand over hers.

When they arrived at Del Porto they were seated and true to his word, the waiter bought them a bottle of good champagne.

"Spoiler alert," teased Judith. "Because you are definitely spoiling me tonight."

"I like spoiling you. And oh, that reminds me. I need to ask you what you think of this thing I got . . ." He patted his pockets, looking for something.

Judith waited for him to find what she assumed was his phone, probably to show her a picture of his latest creation. But just then, a waiter stepped forward, and he was holding Marty's phone up.

She recognized it because she had bought the unique wood-grained phone case for him.

"Look, Marty, he has your phone. Did you drop it? It looks like the waiter found it."

"Yes, I gave it to him," said Marty, reaching inside his inside jacket pocket and finding what he was looking for. The waiter came even closer with Marty's phone, and Marty held something small enclosed in his hands. He suddenly stood up.

"Where are you going?" asked Judith, perplexed.

"I'm not going anywhere," he said and then knelt at Judith's side. The waiter hit the phone's record button and started filming. Every diner's face in the restaurant turned toward them, recognizing what was happening, pointing, and holding their collective breath. Then Marty said, "Judith, you make me so happy, and I hope I make you feel the same way. The only thing that would make me even happier is if you would consent to spend the rest of your life with me. Please say you'll marry me. Please say yes."

Judith was in complete shock. So much so, that the first thing that came to mind was, *"Oh damn, why didn't I wear my sparkly shoes?!"* Her next thought was of the many pairs of eyes on her, most of which were filled with hope for the poor fellow on his knees, waiting for her answer. The third thought went to Brenda and how obviously the woman was after Marty and probably his money as well, which made her burn with indignation. Then she looked into Marty's warm, smiling eyes and then deeper into his loving heart and suddenly heard herself say, "Yes."

Marty quickly slipped a ring on her finger, and the room erupted in applause, laughter, and congratulations. And Judith's fourth thought was, *"What the hell did I just do?"*

“Are you serious? How does it look like I am?”
—Lillian

CHAPTER 25

Dawn and Bea pulled into the hospital parking lot and headed inside the multi-story building. Bea stopped at a nurses' station to inquire about the patient, then they headed straight to her room. They found the door open, but they knocked anyway before entering.

"Knock, knock," called Bea.

"Unless you've got a bottle of Ketel One vodka with you, go away," called a female voice.

Dawn and Bea slowly entered the room and found the woman propped up on a foam wedge, her leg in a cast, her body immobilized by gadgets.

"Hello, Lillian," said Dawn.

"How are you today, dear?" asked Bea.

"Are you serious? How does it look like I am?" asked Lillian, with blatant hostility. "And what could you two possibly want?"

"We just came to see if there was something we could do for you, Lillian," said Bea, her voice gentle.

"We're so sorry this happened to you and Jack," said Dawn.

"Jack and I don't need your pity," snapped Lillian.

Bea could see that Lillian's hostility was already working on Dawn's nerves, so she put a warm hand on her friend's arm to calm her.

Dawn nodded in response, rolled her eyes, and continued, "How is Jack doing?"

At that, Lillian suddenly burst into tears, shocking Bea and Dawn. She was never one to show her vulnerability easily. "He's not doing well at all. He's still unconscious. In a coma, so I'm told. I can't even see him because I'm stuck here and feeling like hell myself."The tears rolled down her pale cheeks.

"I wish I could update that information with better news for you, Lillian, but that's the latest I've heard too. But you know, I've also heard that a coma can be a body's way of shutting down some functions so that others could heal. We need to keep our prayers coming," said Bea.

"Not good enough," snapped Lillian nastily. "I need to talk to Jack. I need to see him. He needs to hear my voice." She turned her head to the wall in quiet despair.

"Lillian, can we do something for you? Do you need someone to go to your house for any reason or check in at the art museum for you?"

"No," she answered. "That's all taken care of. The only thing I need is to talk to my husband."

Dawn suddenly had a flash of an idea. She took hold of Bea's sleeve and started pulling her out of the room, calling over her shoulder, "We'll be back in a little bit, Lillian."

"Please don't," she barked.

She hurried her friend out of the building and back to the car, telling her, "Bea, we got to swing by my house, OK? I've got an idea that might just help Lillian."

"What's on your mind, Dawn?"

"Don't worry, I'm not going to pick up any poison," she said, hurrying.

Bea nudged her friend in the side, "I know you're joking, but you can hardly blame the way she is. She's in pain and worried sick about her husband."

"I don't blame her at all. If I were laid up like that, you can imagine what I'd be like."

"Yes, come to think of it, I can," laughed Bea. "They would probably hear you yelling from your hospital bed all the way across the lake and down in the French Quarter."

Dawn gave a small chuckle and then said seriously, "I sure hope her husband pulls through, Bea. I wouldn't wish that on anyone. I had an idea that might just help, but I need to get something from home."

When they arrived at Dawn's house, she quickly fixed them both some coffee and then left Bea for a moment in the kitchen. "I'll be right back. I've got something in the bedroom I need to get."

Bea couldn't imagine what Dawn wanted to show her. Dawn had a strong element of unpredictability about her that Bea loved. She smiled, thinking about some of her past antics, like the time she hosed down some young men who were hassling Lola. Or the time she surprised them all by renting the Gumbeaux Sistahs Gallery building so she and Judith could go into business together. *"There's no telling what she is going to get from the bedroom. It could be a Dead Sea Scroll. Or an African elephant. It truly could be anything at all."* She chuckled as her imagination ran away with her.

So, she didn't know whether to be surprised or disappointed when Dawn returned and plunked down an old-fashioned, pink landline telephone in front of her, wires unplugged and dangling.

"Well, I wasn't expecting this," said Bea, eyebrows raised. "Not sure how this will help Lillian, though. She has a phone in her hospital room, and she probably has her cell with her as well."

"I guarantee that she doesn't have one of these," said Dawn. "I've never told any of you about this, but this is a magic phone." Bea couldn't help but notice a hint of sadness in Dawn's voice. She glanced at her friend's eyes and saw the pain that was weighing heavily there.

Bea's eyebrows shot up questioningly. "What is this, Dawn? What do you mean 'magic?'"

"I call it a Spirit Phone. Now, I know this may sound crazy, but I keep it in my bedroom nightstand. And on those long, awful nights, and sometimes even during a bad day, I pick up the phone, dial one, and then I talk to Dan. I tell him about my day and how I'm doing. Mostly I tell him how much I miss him."

Bea could see the tears forming in her friend's eyes and felt her own eyes welling up. "I know it must be so hard for you, dear. I think about you all the time and what you're going through. It's still hard for me sometimes, even though it's been so many years since I lost my husband, David."

"Maybe you could get a Spirit Phone too, Bea. I wonder where we could buy some of these old-style phones. I'll bet someone's selling them online somewhere. The thing is, Bea, this has helped me on some of my worst days. Sometimes, I feel like I'm actually talking to Dan."

Bea put a comforting hand on her friend's shoulder.

Dawn rubbed at her eyes, "Told you you'd think I was crazy."

"I think you're amazing, Dawn. Also crazy in so many ways, but not in this one."

Dawn smiled shakily.

"But what about Lillian? How will it help her?" asked Bea.

"Well, I know that her husband is alive, but she can't get to him. It might just make her feel better to pick up the phone and talk to him. We don't really understand all that goes on when someone is in a coma. I like to think we can communicate somehow, and maybe this phone can be a workable tool, at least to make her feel better, maybe. Who knows? We could certainly try."

"I think it's a great idea. Let's bring it to her right now. But if it brings comfort to you, won't you need it, Dawn?"

"Lillian needs it more than I do right this minute. Besides, I can always go buy another phone."

As they were getting back in their car, Dawn said, "There's one thing, Bea. That phone is a wonderful aid to me, but if it ever rings, I will flat-out have a heart attack. If you ever find me dead with the phone in my hand, you'll know what happened."

Bea laughed most of the way to the hospital.

When they arrived back in Lillian's room, they explained the phone to her, adding, "I call it a Spirit Phone. I've been calling my husband, Dan, on it since he passed. I like to dial the number one, and then talk to him. It makes me feel more connected to him."

"Will it spirit you away? If so, then leave it here for me," snapped Lillian. "You two have a lot of nerve bringing this here. In case you haven't heard, my husband isn't dead!"

Dawn winced but Bea explained gently, "Dawn thought that since we don't really understand what it's like to be in a coma, that maybe Jack would be open to a different form of communication while he's unconscious. Maybe he could 'hear' you in a different way."

"Hmph," said Lillian.

"If nothing else," added Dawn, "It might just make you feel a little better."

"You know what would make me feel better? You two leaving me alone. That would be the best medicine I can think of right now." But as she was talking, she tucked the phone under the covers of her bed, out of sight.

Bea winked at Dawn, "Let's let her get some rest, Dawn. Take care, Lillian. We'll come to see you again soon."

Lillian gave the two women a dirty look as they left. But as soon as the door closed behind them, she dug out the phone and, breathing heavily, picked up the receiver and dialed her lucky number—seven. Her voice was shaky as she said, "Jack, it's me," Tears pooled and spilled from her eyes, and she cried out, "Don't you dare leave me, you big oaf. I swear, I'll kill you dead if you do."

"You're a goddess, Lola! A plant-loving, green goddess!"
—Zoe

CHAPTER 26

Lola and Zoe drove to the job site in the morning while it was still cool. Lola drove her truck which was filled with plants, landscaping materials, and tools. When they arrived, she introduced Zoe to the woman who owned the house, "Mrs. Roberts, this is my assistant, Zoe. She'll be helping me out this morning."

Zoe had borrowed some work clothes from Dawn and was ready for the outdoor job. Lola taught her how to dig out areas in the lawn, and together they created a garden across the front of the house that included native plants, pavers, flagstone, and many bags of mulch. It was hard work, but Zoe took a cue from Lola and could tell the older woman had a deep satisfaction from watching the presentation come together.

By the time they finished and were standing in the shade enjoying glasses of Mrs. Robert's iced tea, Zoe was hooked. She loved the satisfaction of creating something beautiful outdoors, and she admired the Zen effect that the work had on her new boss—and mentor. It seemed to Zoe that Lola was one of the easiest people to get along with that she had ever met, not to mention the coolest. Happiness radiated from the older woman, and her tanned, freckled face often held a grin.

As they got in the truck to leave, Lola said, "I need to stop by my family's nursery for a minute on the way home. You don't mind, do you?"

Zoe said she didn't. The truth was she was curious to see more of Lola's life.

Lola's dad, Fred Trahan, was in his eighties and retired, but he still came into the nursery office every day. It wasn't so much to keep an eye on the business as it was to visit and talk to the people he had done business with for decades. When Lola brought Zoe into the main building, her dad sat, holding court behind the main counter. He rose when he saw his daughter and gave her a bear hug in his still-strong arms.

When Lola introduced him to Zoe, he took her hand and shook it firmly, "Young lady, I hope you know what you're doing, hanging out with my crazy daughter." His eyes twinkled with laughter.

Zoe grinned at him and said, "I don't know about crazy, Mr. Trahan, but she sure is talented. I've been working with her all morning, and I have to say that I think I've fallen in love with this business."

Fred took a step back, looking at her hard, and asked, "Love it? Like you might want to go into this business?"

"I haven't thought about it enough, I'll admit, but yes, maybe so," she said, and as she spoke, a light shone in her blue eyes for the first time in months. "I'm supposed to go to school and major in accounting so that I can join my family's accounting firm. Everyone expects it of me. But I'm not sure that is my calling now."

"Now you've done it, Lola," Fred bellowed, winking at his daughter. He turned back to Zoe, "Well, do you want my advice?" he asked.

"Yes, I do," said Zoe sincerely.

"OK, here it is. Go to law school. Then figure out what you want to do. It's the same advice I've given every one of my own kids, and some of them, including Lola here, were smart enough to listen."

Zoe turned to Lola, "You're a lawyer?"

Lola laughed and said, "I'm afraid so."

"Well, I'm impressed," answered Zoe, her eyes wide.

Lola got up and started grabbing some supplies she needed from the nursery with Zoe's help. Soon they were saying goodbye to Fred.

"Mark my words, young lady—law school!" Fred called after them.

When they got outside, Zoe said, "What was that all about? Was he serious about law school?" She was perplexed.

Lola chuckled. "Don't mind my dad. He thinks everyone should go to law school and tells them so too. I'll admit that my law degree comes in handy for me sometimes, especially when it comes to my activism work. But my dad also paid for my education. Not everyone has the luxury or time to pick up a law degree, especially if they have to start their business with student loans. Besides, becoming a landscaper is not dependent on a law degree." She laughed and looked side-eyed at the young woman, "Were you serious about wanting to be a landscaper?"

"Actually, I think I would love it," said Zoe, nodding. "But my parents will kill me. They are really pushing me to join the family business."

"Hmm," thought Lola, "Tell you what, I think your parents are right in some ways."

Zoe looked surprised, "I did not expect you to say that."

"An education is nothing to sneeze at," Lola continued. "But here's what I think. You could start school and study landscape architecture or another related field along with some of your basic courses. Some accounting courses would serve you well no matter what business you go into. Then see how it goes. Meanwhile, you could work for me part-time. That way, you could see if this business is for you."

"Really?" asked Zoe excitedly.

"Sure. You're a good, hard worker, and I could use the help."

"Oh, my word! You're a goddess, Lola! A plant-loving, green goddess! Thank you."

—∞—

When they arrived at Dawn's house, Zoe excused herself to take a shower. Lola sat in Dawn's big kitchen, sharing coffee and talking about their day. Dawn jumped suddenly to her feet and yelled, "Oh no, you didn't, Lola Broussard! You had one day with my granddaughter, and you broke her. My daughters will kill me! They were happy that Zoe was visiting me and hoped that I might inspire her to go ahead with her accounting studies. When Zoe tells them that she is going to study landscaping, heads will roll. I'll get blamed. Shoot, I always get blamed."

"Calm down, Dawn. She hasn't decided yet. We just had a conversation about it, is all. She's a young woman who needs to give her life some thought and do what makes her happy. Doesn't she deserve that?"

"Of course, she does," snapped Dawn. "But my family has a stubborn streak. As in, pack-of-mules stubborn."

"Well, I'll tell you. I think the girl has some talent for the work. And she obviously enjoys it, and she has a real feel for it too. She came up with some ideas this morning I hadn't even thought of. I was impressed."

"Well, let's hope she makes the right decision, and let's hope my family doesn't blame me for whatever it is."

"It'll be fine," nodded Lola.

"Easy for you to say," said Dawn, scowling. "And whatever you do, don't let Zoe near your dad, or she'll end up in law school too."

Lola rolled her eyes, laughing, "Oh, Dad's already had a crack at her."

Dawn groaned.

"Shoot! If I had known that,
I would have started inviting felons over for barbecues at our place way before this."
—Bud

CHAPTER 27

Bud and Lola pulled up in front of Mrs. Albertson's house, just up the street from Bud's nursery.

As they walked to the front door, Bud whispered apologetically, "Thanks again for coming with me. Her daughter, Doris, said her mother was thrilled we could make it for lunch. Apparently, Mrs. Albertson doesn't get many visitors these days. Doris sounded very grateful."

"It's so like you to be having lunch with an eighty-five-year-old customer who is also a known thief. It's one of the many reasons I love you. Remind me to thank you for that later this evening." She winked at him suggestively.

"Shoot! If I had known that, I would have started inviting felons over for barbecues at our place way before this." he said, chuckling.

Lola laughed and hugged his arm as he rang the front doorbell. They heard the door start to open, and Bud quickly whispered to Lola, "By the way, I should mention that the old lady has a bit of a crush on me."

"What? Yeah, you probably should have mentioned that," said Lola sarcastically. She gave his arm a playful punch.

Mrs. Albertson's daughter Doris opened the door and welcomed them inside. After introductions, she said, "She's so excited to share her world with you, Bud. Um, you too, Lola. Let me just go get mom." She walked down the hall, calling for her mother.

"Her world?" whispered Lola to Dan, "That's an odd way to describe a house, don't you think?" She raised her eyebrows questioningly.

Mrs. Albertson ambled in from the kitchen with a wide grin and sparkling old blue eyes, "Oh my goodness! I'm so happy you could come, Bud. Come on back with me. And you too, Mrs. Broussard. We'll have lunch in the sunroom."

Lola and Bud followed the older woman and her daughter through the large, old-fashioned kitchen with its beadboard walls and cast-iron sink and into a small, sun-drenched room lined with bakers' racks filled with green, healthy house plants. In the middle sat an oak table with a milk glass vase brimming with blue hydrangeas.

Lola stood still and took in the little room. "Mrs. Albertson, this is possibly the most inviting room I've ever been in."

"Thank you, dear," said Mrs. Albertson. "How about you call me Vera?"

"You should give them a tour of Veraland before lunch," suggested Doris.

"Veraland?" asked Bud with an amused glint in his eyes.

"That's right," said Vera, quite seriously, pointing to a sign over the door leading to the backyard that spelled out in cursive "Welcome to Veraland."

Lola was delighted, "I would love to see Veraland."

"I had a feeling you might. Bud told me that you are a landscaper, and of course, he owns my favorite nursery. I don't let just anyone into Veraland, you know."

"She really doesn't," confirmed Doris. "It's her little private Shangri-La. By invitation only."

"I'd be honored," said Lola sincerely.

Vera stepped up close to Bud and took hold of his arm. She looked up into his eyes and said, "How about you, Bud. Would you like to see more of Vera? I mean, Veraland." She batted her eyes mischievously.

Doris hooted in laughter, "Leave the poor man alone, Mom."

"Well then," said Mrs. Albertson. "Shall we?" She held the door open for her guests, and they stepped out onto a small porch where she joined them.

Both Bud and Lola stood on the porch with their mouths open and took it all in. Everywhere they looked, every which way they turned, there was another exquisite display of plants and flowers, from the commonplace to the exotic. The collection went up the sides of the house, carport, and garage with netting covering half the yard providing shade where needed and allowing for sun where it was not. There were decades of work represented here, and it was executed perfectly.

"Oh, Vera!" said Lola, breathing it all in. "Veraland is just beautiful." She glanced at Bud, who looked just as astonished as she felt.

"I had no idea that you were such a master gardener, Vera," he said.

"Thank you, dear," said Vera, preening and accepting the compliment as her due.

"She's amazing, isn't she?" asked Doris.

"Where did you get all this, Vera?" asked Bud, intrigued about some plants that were unfamiliar, even to him.

"This house belonged to my mom and dad, and I inherited it and all this. They were good gardeners in their time, and they started by growing food in raised beds back here. But when I was a teenager, I caught the bug and started adding to the collection. Many of my plants were given to me by friends, or I bought them, or . . ." She hesitated here. "Or they came from other places."

"Apparently, you stole some of them, Mom," said Doris. "Just admit it."

"I will not," said Mrs. Albertson stubbornly, lifting her chin with a frown for her daughter.

Doris went on, "Her dad named it Veraland at some point and put up that sign for her. She does all the work herself still, can you believe it? She tried to pass the bug along to me, but it didn't stick. But I'm good for grunt labor. She won't let me plant or trim anything, but I'm allowed to water sometimes."

"Well, it's not Dorisland, is it?" asked Mrs. Albertson snippily.

"This is absolutely amazing, Vera. Honestly, I could spend hours back here, and I know I could learn a lot from you. A lot of people would love to know what you know about plants," enthused Lola.

"Shoot, you could teach a class in this if you wanted to," added Bud.

"I would love to teach a class," said Vera. "And I'd be great at it too."

"My mother is so modest," smiled Doris.

"The trouble is that I really don't like having visitors in here. It's a sanctuary to me. My spiritual home."

"I don't blame you, really," nodded Bud.

"But you are welcome here anytime, Bud," she said with a toothy smile.

"You know I wish you would consider teaching a class, mom. I know you'd love it, and it might keep you out of trouble," said Doris, rolling her eyes.

The old woman responded with a hasty, "I think it's time for lunch."

As Bud and Lola got into their car to go home, Lola said, "That woman is a shaman. I can't believe the gift she has. And Veraland is a monument to her genius." Then she added teasingly, "I'm so glad I got to see this, even if it does cost me a husband."

"Not this week. Especially since I'm about to get lucky tonight. Don't think I forgot," he grinned at her.

Lola laughed, taking his arm affectionately. She added seriously, "You know, it's a shame to keep a talent like that to herself."

"I'm stunned at what she's done in that backyard. I hope we can visit again sometime."

"I believe she'd let you come over any time," laughed Lola, "I'll just be lucky if she lets me come too."

"Don't be making me laugh when I'm furious with you!"
—Judith

CHAPTER 28

Just as she had been for the last few days, Judith was distracted as she drove Pauline to the Gumbeaux Sistahs Gallery for her first visit. All Judith had been able to think about recently was Marty's proposal. It had floored her, but she knew it was a proposition worth considering. Marty was such a good man. He was kind and funny, and he had those warm, friendly, brown eyes that she loved. He made her feel special. There was no question that she loved him and that he was a great catch. Any woman would be happy to have him. *"Especially Brenda,"* she thought.

"But do I really want to get married? And what if that woman steals him from me because I won't be his wife?" she wondered in alarm. Her panic suddenly felt out of control, and she found herself whispering fiercely out loud, "Oh my Lord, no! I'll marry you!"

"Uh, no thanks, Miss Judith," answered Pauline, wide-eyed. "Don't get me wrong—you're a fine lady, alright, but if Pauline is going to get married, she's gonna marry a rich, old man with a bad cough. Know what I mean?" She cackled loudly.

Red-faced and flustered, Judith pulled up in front of the gallery, saying, "Oh, don't mind me, Pauline. I'm flat-out crazy over that proposal from Marty."

"Oh gotcha," answered Pauline, nodding. "Well, if you ask me, you should say yes to that one. He's a whole lot on the yummy side."

"I've just got to think about it," said Judith, opening the car door.

"Don't think too long, or someone will snatch him away like a pearl necklace," warned Pauline.

As Judith unlocked the front door, she pointed out the Friendship Bench in front of the gallery to Pauline. "Occasionally, you'll see someone walk up and sit on that bench, and that means that they need to talk to someone. The sistahs and I take turns on a schedule, meeting and talking to people on the bench. Today is Helen's turn, so she'll be here shortly."

"That's real kind of y'all," said Pauline. "Y'all are good women, that's for sure."

"It's very rewarding, actually. It's improved my life a great deal to help others around me." They walked inside the gallery, and she said, "So, come on in, Pauline, and I'll show you around."

"This place is pretty, Miss Judith."

Judith pointed out where the kitchen and bathroom were located and where they kept the cleaning supplies. Pauline was going to work that morning by cleaning up the gallery. Judith explained the cafe area where coffee and pastries were sold. She also showed her the artwork by various artists. Lastly, she showed her the main desk and checkout.

Just when Pauline started pulling out the duster and vacuum, Judith's cell phone rang. When she answered it and listened a moment, her voice rose to a high pitch as she said, "Oh no! I'm so sorry. Can you hold onto her for a few minutes, please? I'll be right there!"

She hung up and grabbed her keys and purse. "What's happening?" asked Pauline.

"Lucy got out of the yard again, and my next-door neighbor, Millie, found her eating her cats' food on her patio. She got her to come inside her house, but I've got to get over there and save her."

"Save Lucy?"

"Oh heavens no. I've got to go and save Millie from that crazy pug of mine. Millie is no spring chicken, and Lucy's liable to be jumping all over her because she's so happy to see a new face."

"What should I do?" asked Pauline.

"Just mind the place for a few minutes. I'll be right back. If anyone comes in, tell them I'll be here in ten minutes."

"Ok, got it, boss," nodded Pauline seriously, "You can count on me."

Judith picked up her little pug from Millie's house and carried her back home. "Lucy, it's a good thing I like you so much, you bad little thing." She fussed at the dog as the dog barked, spun around, and licked her face. Judith couldn't help but laugh. "Don't be making me laugh when I'm furious with you!" she said.

She put the little dog into the house, saying, "It's a pretty day, but you'll have to stay inside until I can get back here and figure out how you escaped. I have a sneaking suspicion that you dug up that hole I filled in last week."

She shut the door, jumped in her car, and hurried back to the gallery. As she pulled up, she spotted two women on the Friendship Bench in front. She thought at first one of the women must be Helen come to take her turn on the bench. But to her sudden horror, she realized that it was not Helen talking to the second woman whom she recognized as Mrs. Allen. Just last week, Judith had sat and talked with Mrs. Allen, who was dealing with a cheating husband.

"Oh no, no, no!" repeated Judith, as she jumped from the car and hurried across the street to the bench.

"Hi there," said Pauline, looking up and smiling.

Mrs. Allen suddenly jumped to her feet, saying, "I've just got to run now. Good to see you, Judith, and it certainly was good to meet you, Pauline. And thanks so much for the talk. I wish someone had given me this advice months ago when Freddie started fooling around with that awful librarian. I believe that thing you suggested is the only way I'm going to feel better about all this, and that's a fact!"

As Mrs. Allen hurried down the street, Judith turned her wide eyes to Pauline, "Oh my Lord, Pauline! You're not supposed to work the Friendship Bench! That takes some training! We have rules involved. What advice did you give her?"

"Just common sense, really. It's stuff every woman should know about a low-down cheater."

Judith felt her panic rising, "Like what?"

"Oh, you know. I told her that when he comes home next time from being out late with his girlfriend, she should be waiting for him with a big stick, or a fireplace poker, or a taser if she can find one. I got one of those around here somewhere—she can borrow mine. Also, she might need a knife . . ."

Judith let out a big yelp and ran inside to dig her phone out of her purse. She found Mrs. Allen's number and got her on the phone as Pauline wandered in and listened.

It took about ten minutes, but Judith was able to convince Mrs. Allen that Pauline was not supposed to be working the bench, and if she followed her advice, she would end up in jail and probably charged with a felony. She told her that what she probably needed to do was talk things out with her husband and for her to make up her mind if she even wanted to be in that relationship.

"Well, maybe you're right, Judith," said Mrs. Allen reluctantly. "But I swear I'm inspired just to be tough like Pauline and stand up for myself. I'm not going to take his cheating anymore. I'm done. And for once, I feel pretty damn good about myself."

"That's good news, Mrs. Allen. Just leave off the taser, OK? Now you come back anytime and visit us on the bench anytime you want."

When she got off the phone, Pauline said, "You told her to talk it out with him? I'd say the talking was done with. If that's the kind of advice you give, well, I can see that I'm gonna be needed around here." She gave Judith a nod that said "I-mean-business" and went off to the supply closet in search of the cleanser.

"Can you imagine if
Dawn made all of our life decisions?"
—Lola

CHAPTER 29

"And then she told Mrs. Allen to lie in wait for her husband with a taser!" said Judith, slapping the table, still unbelieving over the events as she related them to the sistahs at their next meeting.

"Oh my God," said Trinity, who had made the trek over the Causeway bridge to attend this meeting at the gallery. She loved any chance to see her sistahs. "Poor Mrs. Allen! And poor you, Judith! You must've had a heart attack."

"And that's not the worst of it," confided Judith, rolling her eyes and wiping the perspiration building up on her forehead just thinking of the ordeal. "Ever since then, a whole slew of newcomers has shown up at the bench, requesting to talk to Pauline! Apparently, she is now a superstar with the unfaithful spouse and divorce crowd."

"It's probably a good thing she didn't try and give me advice over Harry's infidelity. I would love to have permission to taser that man. Just the thought of it is so very satisfying," Trinity said with a wild look in her eyes.

"Oh dear," said Bea. "You don't mean that, Trinity."

Trinity shrugged, making it clear that she might. Bea grabbed the moment to move on. "We can't let this happen, Judith. If any of those women follow through on her advice, we'll have a bunch of people in pain, and that probably makes us accessories to a crime."

Lola and Dawn could not stop giggling over the whole thing. Dawn said, "Next thing you know, she'll be giving streetwalking lessons to the divorcees."

Lola was holding her sides, laughing, "I can see the headlines. 'The Gumbeaux Sistahs Gallery implicated in rising crime rate.'"

"Or how about—Sex Worker Sting at Local Art Gallery!" suggested Dawn, helpless with laughter.

Judith groaned loudly.

Bea tried to get the meeting back on track, "Apparently, Pauline could use some training in non-felonious advice. Tell you what, Helen and I will come to visit her this afternoon and do a mini training. Then we'll sit with her for her first few times on the bench."

"You think she should still sit out there?" exclaimed Judith, her eyes wide.

"We can't stop her from giving advice out, but we can sure push her gently away from getting the local women locked up with her advice. And if she is as popular with these newcomers as you say, she might just be able to do some good. Maybe we could use it to help those who might not have shown up on the bench otherwise."

Judith looked skeptical, but Trinity spoke up, "I think it might work, Judith. That woman has her heart in the right place. Her mouth is still stuck on Bourbon Street, but maybe we can work with that."

"Well, OK," said Judith. "But please do accompany her for a while."

"Of course, dear," said Bea confidently. "We'll come see her this afternoon at your place—the sooner, the better, I think. Trinity, why don't you stop in at the house too and say hello to Pauline. I'm sure she'd love to see you, and she respects your opinion."

Bea continued, "And now let's move one, shall we? We have a lot to talk about today. Trinity, I'm sure glad you're back to normal."

"Yes, I'm still shaking every time I think about getting arrested. Those policemen should have known better. Harry and I have donated heavily to the policemen's fund, for heaven's sake. They should know I'm no streetwalker."

Dawn looked at Trinity's outfit that she chose for this morning's meeting. Her clothes tended to be on the flamboyant and sexy side. She said with a snigger, "How could they tell?" she joked.

Trinity smacked her sister with an empty paper plate that moments before held one of Helen's croissants. Crumbs flew everywhere, which sent Lola into more gales of laughter.

"Be nice," warned Trinity. "Besides, it turns out that my being arrested had a bright side. I got ahold of the judge that will be arraigning Pauline when her case comes up. I was able to put in a good word for her. The judge is an old friend of Harry's and has been at our house a couple of times for dinner. He didn't discuss the case with me, but he was impressed that Pauline now has employment with the gallery."

"Well, good. Let's help her keep going then," said Dawn. "I like Pauline. She makes me laugh—a lot. That goes a long way with me these days."

"And that brings us to you, Dawn. What's happening with you? We've all been thinking about you, and if you need us in any way, please let us know. In fact, Lola, I'm counting on you to intuit Dawn's needs and let us know even before she knows what they are."

Lola patted Dawn's arm, "She knows I'm there for her."

Dawn smiled and said, "Thanks, y'all. Bea, I know you will tell them about our hospital patient when it's your turn, so right now I'm just gonna mention that Lola has ruined my life."

"Oh boy," said Bea, laughing. "What did you do, Lola?"

Dawn went on, "My daughters are going to kill me. In fact, my whole family will kill me. You know they're all looking forward to the day that Zoe gets out of school and joins the family accounting firm. Well, Lola upped and invited Zoe to a landscaping job and then convinced her to study landscape architecture in school. It's all she can talk about. I'm gonna be very, very dead when they all find out."

"That's wonderful news!" said Helen, smiling. "Not the dead part but the fact that she found her calling."

"No, no calling!" groaned Dawn.

"She's really a natural at it," nodded Lola. "She has a feel for working with nature and not fighting against it. She gets it."

Dawn wailed, "Do you get that I'm dead, Lola?"

"Death by college major. I never heard of that one," laughed Lola.

"That girl has to let her heart lead her, and you know it, Dawn," said Trinity.

"I know, I know," said Dawn miserably. "I guess it's just a change we're gonna have to face."

Helen spoke up, "I wish Zoe would change her opinion about Coop. It's amazing how much they antagonize each other. Coop can't say anything nice about Zoe."

Dawn complained, "Yeah, it's the same on this end with Zoe."

"Well, they don't have to spend any time together, thank goodness. I'm afraid the fur will fly if they do."

"The two of them have college and life decisions to make right now. You would think they'd be friends. They have things in common," said Judith.

"They don't have to be friends," said Bea. "But, of course, it's kind of a shame. And speaking of shame—Lola, how is it that you and Judith have planned this big fundraising event for Safe House, and no one has asked for the sistahs' help yet?"

Lola chuckled, "Oh, don't worry. I was just waiting my turn. So, Judith has been working on her old paintings like a crazy person, and I've got the social media plan and flyers ready to roll out. I'm gonna need all the help we can get with ticket sales and distributing the art to the sponsoring businesses and getting the closing party to come together."

"When's the event?" asked Helen.

"It's coming up in a few weeks. Can I count on you sistahs to help?"

"You know you can," said Helen.

"How's the painting coming along, Judith?" asked Lola, "Judith is getting her old paintings ready to donate to the treasure hunt. She's got quite a collection. It's so wonderful of her to do this. We have to sing praises loud and long about her work and give her lots of publicity. It's the least we can do."

"It's a win-win. Those old paintings have been hanging around forever. I get my house and studio cleaned up, Safe House gets money, and the gallery gets the publicity. Happy Campers, all."

"Well, that does sound like a good deal. And of course we'll help, Judith. Do you have anything more to talk about?"

"There is one little thing," said Judith, grimacing.

"What's up?" asked Helen.

"Well, OK. I didn't know whether to bring it up, but well . . ." she stammered.

"Whoo boy!" said Dawn. "I don't know what you're trying to say, but if it's got you this tongue-tied, it's gotta be something good. Out with it!"

Flummoxed, Judith blurted, "OK, OK. It's just that . . . Marty asked me to marry him."

Dawn's mouth fell open, "What? Oh my—that is good!"

Lola jumped to her feet, clapping, "Oh, that's fantastic, sistah! You're going to love it. I'm so glad I married Dan. Best thing I ever did—twice!"

"We're so happy for you," cried Helen and Trinity.

Bea was the only one keeping quiet as she observed her friend's worried expression. Then she asked, "What did you tell him, Judith?"

"She said yes, of course," said Dawn. Then she stopped and turned towards Judith, "Wait. You did say yes, right?"

"I did say yes, but then I told him afterward that I had to think about it."

"Seriously?" asked Dawn, shocked. "What's wrong with you? Marty's such a good guy!"

"He's perfect for you. No way is he the type to run off with his assistant, you know?" asked Trinity.

"Why, what did you hear?" asked Judith, alarmed.

"Nothing! I just said that because that's what my Harry did." Then she asked, "You love him, don't you?"

"Yes, I do. I love him very much."

"Then, what's the problem?" asked Lola.

"Now, dear, we're old enough to know that being in love with someone is not the only consideration when it comes to marriage," said Bea.

"I don't know. I think it's a hell of a good start," enthused Dawn sarcastically.

"Bea's right," answered Helen. "You need to think about whether or not you value the same things. Also, you need life goals that match up."

"And whether or not he likes to sleep with his damned assistants," added Trinity.

They all looked at Judith expectantly, who squirmed uncomfortably. She both regretted bringing up the subject and wished fervently that she could talk her way into a solution with the sistahs.

Finally, Bea said, "Well, dear, you are smart to take your time with this. It's a big step. I have confidence in your decision, Judith, and if you want to talk, just say the word to any of us. You know that."

"Or, if you want to just leave your life up to me, then I'll make the decisions for you right here and now," laughed Dawn and the sistahs joined in.

"Oh my God, can you imagine if Dawn made all our life decisions?" said Lola, laughing loudly. "We'd all end up working in the circus or living in Paris. Wait, come to think of it, that sounds like fun!"

"See?" said Dawn smugly. "Just say the word."

"Not gonna happen, sistah," said Judith. "I'm in enough trouble. And it's more than just whether or not I want to be married again, although that's the main problem. I have a problem with Marty's assistant, Brenda. She flirts with him like crazy!"

"I knew it!" said Trinity. "Seriously, let me at her! Enough with the assistants already!"

"Calm down, Trin," said Dawn. "We don't have all the facts yet. Like whether Marty is flirting back or not. And if he is, then we'll just have to dispose of him."

"Or tell Pauline about him." said Lola, laughing.

"Oh my Lord, whatever you do, don't tell Pauline about this!" yelped Judith. "She'll whip out a Taser on the spot. Poor Marty wouldn't stand a chance!"

"Well, how is Marty handling it?" asked Bea, seriously.

"He acts like it's nothing really. Like he doesn't even notice it. But I sure notice it!"

"Oh dear," said Trinity. "Marty is such a nice man. I would hate to have to ice the guy."

Bea cleared her throat and gave Trinity a stern look.

"I mean, send him away on a nice long journey from which he never returns," amended Trinity.

"Y'all are a big help," groaned Judith.

"You obviously need to talk to Marty to set your mind at ease," said Helen nodding sagely and the sistahs murmured their agreement.

"I guess you're right. I just feel kind of silly—being jealous at my age. "

"It's not silly. It's a weird problem to have at any age," said Lola. "Let us know what you decide though, Judith. We'll support you no matter what."

"OK, let's get back on track," smiled Bea. "Dawn, why don't you catch the girls up on our patient."

"Sure. Lillian is a mess," started Dawn. "I feel so bad for her. She's got broken bones, she's stuck in the hospital, and the most horrible thing of all is that her husband, Jack, is still in a coma from the accident."

"Oh heavens," said Helen. "We've all been praying for her."

"I know. We've had our run-ins with that woman, but I wouldn't wish this on my worst enemy. Actually, she *is* my worst enemy," said Lola, thinking of how Lillian had once gotten Judith fired and then tried to take credit for Lola's work. "Of course," she thought, "I did sleep with her husband that one time." Lola's cheeks burned with shame as they did every time she thought about her indiscretion during a bad period in her life.

Judith added, "I know she got me fired from the museum and tried to sabotage our gallery opening, and she hasn't exactly been a dream to be around, but praying is the least we can do."

"We can do more," said Bea firmly. "Dawn and I have been visiting, and Dawn even had a wonderful idea for Lillian."

Dawn told them about the Spirit Phone and how she had uses it to call Dan at night when she feels alone and heartbroken.

Judith reached out to her partner and laid a hand on her shoulder, "You're not ever alone, Dawn. You have us anytime you need us. Even late at night if you need to talk."

"Oh, I know, but you know what I mean," said Dawn, blinking back tears.

"I think your Spirit Phone is a wonderful idea," chimed in Trinity. "But Lillian is not a widow. So how does that work?"

"I know, but because Jack is in a coma, it might just work for her."

"I'd like to borrow that phone sometime," said Helen. "Do you think I could use it to call my ex-husband? He might be gone, but I'd still like to give him a piece of my mind."

"You do realize that it's not just that phone that does the trick, right? Any phone will work. It's just a tool to help people feel better," said Dawn.

"Says you," insisted Helen.

"Well, how about we all pay a visit to Lillian? It might help. We can go one at a time or all together."

"Why don't we just call her on that phone?" laughed Trinity.

Bea gave her that look that could silence the lambs. She continued, "How about Thursday?"

“Zoe, why are you trying to prune that man’s hair?”
—Lola

CHAPTER 30

Zoe pulled in front of the Gumbeaux Sistahs Gallery. The back seat of her car was covered with some new garden tools that she could not resist buying. She had a new pair of loppers in the mix that she couldn't wait to show Lola because she had nicknamed it Cindy Lopper. She knew Lola would get a kick out of that. But that would have to wait. She was at the gallery to pick up her grandmother, Dawn. They agreed to have lunch together today at the English Tea Room after the sistahs' meeting. She texted Dawn as the Gumbeaux Sistah meeting was ending to tell her she was waiting out front. She settled down with her phone to wait.

She glanced up from the screen for a moment, and her face fell. "Oh, brother," she whispered to herself. "I hope he doesn't see me."

Cooper walked up the sidewalk on the other side of the street in front of the gallery.

As Zoe watched, trying to scrunch down in her seat, a tan-colored van pulled up alongside Cooper. He stopped on the sidewalk, scowling, as he peered into the van windows. The driver of that car rolled down the window and was saying something to Cooper. She couldn't hear what it was, but she was shocked when Cooper suddenly turned red with anger and began shouting at the driver. The driver's door burst open, and a tall, lanky, rough-looking man jumped out of the van and ran up to Cooper and punched him hard in the side of his head.

Zoe's mouth fell open, and she yelled loudly, "No! Leave him alone!"

The man stood over Cooper and punched him again. Then he began to drag the teenager towards the still-running car.

Before she even had time to think about it, Zoe jumped from her car and ran screaming across the street.

"Leave him alone!"

The man looked up just in time to find a strange, young woman barreling into him and knocking him over. Then he found a large pair of garden loppers opened near his face.

"What are you doing, Zoe?" croaked Cooper from the sidewalk. "Get away from him. He's crazy and dangerous."

"He may be dangerous, but Cindy Lopper is about to make him ugly too!" screamed Zoe to the prone man.

". . . Cindy Lopper?" asked Cooper and started to chuckle despite the awful pain in his head.

At that point, all the commotion on the sidewalk brought the sistahs tumbling out through the gallery doors.

"What the hell?" screamed Dawn.

"Zoe, why are you trying to prune that man's hair?" asked Lola, aghast.

"Oh my God," said Helen. "It's Andre. Coop's stepfather. He's out of jail."

"I'm here to get my boy back," yelled Andre. "Get off of me." He was yelling that last part at Dawn, who sat down on his legs as Zoe continued to wield the loppers threateningly. Bea called the police.

"Why do you want him back?" asked an angry Helen. "So you can keep beating him?"

"What's wrong with you, man? Who beats their kid like that?" asked Lola, looking from the injured young man on the ground to his fuming stepfather, itching to give the latter a good kick in the ass.

As the police drove up, Andre looked up at Helen and said, "Look, lady. I know who you are, and you can't have my boy. I still have rights. I'm his father."

"You're nobody's father," hissed Dawn.

Two policemen walked up, and Dawn yelled out, "I'm making a sistah's arrest, officer!"

When the police learned what had happened, they hauled Andre to his feet and started to lead him off to their patrol car. Andre looked at the group with a big, crazy grin that did not reach his eyes, "Boy! Papa will be back. Count on it."

One of the policemen introduced himself as Sergeant Jeffers. He asked Cooper if he was alright. The young man insisted that he did not need to go to the hospital even though he had a pretty good shiner starting to bloom. The policemen put Andre into their car and drove off. The sistahs and Zoe tended to Cooper.

He sat on the Friendship Bench, and the sistahs headed back inside to find him some ice and a cold drink. Zoe hesitated a moment, then joined him on the bench.

"Sure you're OK?" she asked.

"I've had worse," he mumbled. Then he looked directly at Zoe and nodded. "Thanks for bringing out the pop star."

"The what?"

"You know, Cindy Lopper," He broke into a grin, "That was pretty good."

"Oh," she laughed. "I didn't think anyone had heard that."

"I did, and thanks," he said, eyeing her. "I think I was more surprised than Andre. You can really handle your garden tools."

She looked at him seriously. "What are you going to do now?" she asked.

"What can I do? Now that he's out, I probably have a couple of days till he makes bail and is out on the streets again. He's a pig-headed ass, and he doesn't like to lose. That's what this is all about—being in control of me. I know that he thinks this is some sort of battle and that he's lost a few rounds. He's good for his word on this. He'll be back."

"You have to make sure he doesn't win, Coop. Miss Helen can help you. Maybe you should let her adopt you. Let a judge take you away from him for good. He's such a bad person! I can't believe he'd just beat up his own kid like that!"

"I'm not beaten up. I've just been sucker-punched a few times. I'm OK."

"Who's pig-headed now?" she asked with a grin, and he couldn't help but laugh.

"Yeah, maybe," he said, then suddenly turned serious. "Zoe, you don't know me, and maybe we got off on the wrong foot. I still think you're an entitled little brat, but you're a warrior with a pair of loppers. I gotta respect that. I'd hate to see what you could do with a post hole digger."

She chuckled and then smiled at him encouragingly so he would keep talking.

"But here's the thing. You saw a little about where I came from today. I've lost a lot in my life, and if there's one thing I've learned, it's that everything can disappear at any given moment. Miss Helen is wonderful to me. She's probably the only person since my mom died that gave a damn about me. But I just can't lose anything more. I just can't do it."

Zoe thought she'd never seen such a deep sadness brimming out of another human being. "You wouldn't lose her. She loves you, Coop. Don't you know that? All those women in that gallery love you."

"I know, but they're good people. They've seen me be rude, I guess, but I've done some pretty bad stuff they don't know about, Zoe. I've stolen stuff and gotten in fights and broken into houses and . . . well, if they knew . . ."

"Coop, weren't you a kid just trying to survive your horrible situation?"

"Yeah, mostly, I guess," he admitted, "But . . ."

Zoe stopped him, "Miss Helen knows all that."

"Yeah, but I'm such a screw-up," he said, shaking his head. "I know that if I did one more thing—just one more—that they would all see me for who I am. No, it's better just to stay put and lay low till I can get out on my own, which won't be long. Then, I'll move on."

"You're afraid of being left, but you're so willing to do that to them. They don't deserve that. And neither do you. Nobody wants that."

Cooper got to his feet, "Look, Zoe, I know you helped me out, and I thank you. Really, I do. But you don't know what you're talking about."

And just like that, the walls went back up, and Cooper walked away down the street holding his head.

—∞—

The sistahs huddled around the coffee pot in the gallery after the police left.

"What are we going to do about this?" asked Bea, her usually unlined face held an uncommonly worried look.

"I wish that boy would choose to be adopted," said Lola. "It would settle this legal guardianship once and for all."

"I know. I do worry that he'll be sent back to live with that monster if he doesn't.

"It's time to go and talk to the judge again," said Helen firmly. "And to Coop too. He's so stubborn about this."

—∞—

Zoe pushed open the gallery front door and stuck her head inside. Spotting Dawn across the room, she called, "Mamere, can I talk to you outside a moment?"

"Of course," said Dawn, her curiosity peaked. She stepped outside and joined her granddaughter on the Friendship Bench. "What's up?" she asked.

"Well, I know that this is not my business, but I wanted to talk to you about something important."

Dawn was now bursting with curiosity. Her granddaughter was acting so mysterious, so she knew this had to be good. "Out with it, Zoe. You can tell me anything."

Zoe then explained what was on her mind. When she finished stating her case, Dawn threw her hands in the air and exclaimed, "You're a genius, granddaughter! And a sweetheart too. Of course, it's what we should do. I just wish I had thought of it."

Zoe smiled and said, "Thank you, Mamere."

"But listen, let's keep this decision a secret, OK? If the sistahs find out, it will get back to everyone we ever knew and everyone we will know ten years into the future!"

"You got it." She leaned over and gave her grandmother a massive hug that left both of them smiling with tears in Dawn's eyes.

"Are the Gumbeaux Sistahs on a crime-busting spree today?"
—Sergeant Jeffers

CHAPTER 31

When Judith returned home, Trinity and Dawn followed her there to stop in and say hello to Pauline. They pulled up in front of the house, and Judith noticed that the front door was wide open.

"That's weird," she thought, then said aloud, "Pauline must have stepped out into the side garden for a moment."

But as she was getting out of the car, Pauline came running towards her from the side of the house.

By this time, Trinity and Dawn had joined her, saying, "Hey there, Pauline."

But Pauline's demeanor was anything but friendly. She looked terrified.

"Oh lord, he's coming for me!"

"What? Who's coming?" asked Judith, looking around.

Just then, a silver SUV turned the corner fast and came screeching up to their driveway.

"It's Benny!" screamed Pauline. "Hide me! He called me a little while ago and told me that if I didn't come back and work for him that he was going to hurt you, Miss Judith. I think he somehow got ahold of Miss Trinity's address and has been following her. He must have followed you this morning."

Judith already had her phone out and called the police as Benny stalked out of his shiny car.

"The police are on their way!" yelled Trinity.

Benny ignored her and yelled loudly, "Pauline, you get your big ass in that car! You got no business with these people. Like you belong here? C'mon! You need to get back to New Orleans with me. You know I always take care of you. Just try and put that stuff of yours in the streets in this little town—you gonna wind up in some dumpy little jail, and no one can help you here."

"No! I'm done with that," screamed Pauline. "You take care of me? Are you serious? You call black eyes and broken ribs taking care of someone? You are nothing but a crazy person!"

"What else you gonna do then? Flip burgers?"

"If I have to, but I don't have to because I'm a counselor here."

Judith, Dawn, and Trinity turned to look at her, eyebrows raised high.

"Counselor? What are you counseling? Did you open a sex worker school in Covington?" He thought his joke was hilarious and opened his mouth wide, laughing.

Dawn couldn't help but snort out a tiny laugh as well, and Trinity gave her a dirty look.

"Never mind who I'm counseling or what I'm doing," said Pauline. "I'm helping folks is what I'm doing. And I like it."

"Just get in the car, Pauline," he said wearily. "It took me a while to find you, and I don't intend to lose you again. You're my best girl."

Pauline looked at him sadly, "Look, Benny, I once thought you was the best thing that ever happened to me. But I was so wrong."

A police car pulled up to the curb, and the same officer who had responded to Cooper's assault got out. He noticed Judith and Trinity standing there and took a beat. "Are you kidding me, Ladies? Are the Gumbeaux Sistahs on a crime-busting spree today? You ladies should get yourselves your own reality TV show."

"I'm afraid trouble is following us today, Sergeant Jeffers," said Judith apologetically.

"So, what's the trouble here?" he asked, looking around. His gaze fell on Benny, who said calmly, "Ain't no trouble here, officer."

Sergeant Jeffers turned to Pauline and asked, "Is that right, ma'am? Do we have trouble here or not?"

Pauline looked meaningfully at Benny and said, "I don't know, Benny, do we? Now look, I'm sorry you went through all this trouble to find me. I didn't ask to be found. I don't want to be found. I'm really done with you. I'm not coming back." She looked at him firmly, but there was a hint of sadness in her eyes as well.

Benny looked from Pauline to the policeman and said, "Alright, Pauline. I think you're making a huge mistake. You don't know nothing, and you can't do nothing right. But alright. I'm done with you too. You ain't nothing."

"Then maybe you should just get in your car and leave now, sir," said the Sergeant.

"I'm gone," said Benny. He stalked back to his car and took off.

"Thanks, Sergeant Jeffers," said Trinity and Judith. Dawn waved gaily, and Pauline let out a breath of relief.

"No problem. If you have more trouble with him, let me know," said the big officer with a twinkle in his eyes. Then with a smile he said, "But that's it for today, ladies. You've reached your crime-solving quota for the day."

"Let's hope you're right," laughed Judith.

As the Sergeant pulled away, Judith turned to Pauline, "Do you think Benny will be back?"

"I don't know, Miss Judith. It worries me."

"Well, we'll have to deal with that then. I'm not sure you're safe here now. He knows where you are."

"I wouldn't want anything to happen to you because of me, Miss Judith."

Dawn interrupted by asking, "Pauline, did you mean what you said? Because if you did, it gives me an idea."

"What did I say?"

"About wanting to help people?"

"I want *her* to come with me."
—Lillian

CHAPTER 32

The following morning Bea, Dawn, Trinity, Bitsy, and Pauline met at the hospital. Bitsy carried a potted plant for Lillian as they made their way to her room for a visit.

"Oh, lucky me," said Lillian grumpily when they knocked and entered.

"Lillian, you haven't met Pauline yet. She's staying with Judith for a while," said Bea.

"How you doing, Miss Lillian? Is there anything I can do for you?" asked Pauline.

"Yes, can you figure out a way to get these people out of here?"

"Now, now. I know you're just not feeling well right now," said Pauline sympathetically. "But these ladies are super nice. Here, let me plump your pillow and help you with your glass of water."

Lillian stared at the other woman for a moment as Pauline said, "There now. That pillow is nice and soft now. You just lie back, and we'll have us a nice visit." Amazingly, Lillian seemed to relax into Pauline's ministrations.

"Lillian," Bea said, "We were wondering if you'd been able to get in to see Jack yet?"

"Do I look like I've been anywhere?" she snapped.

Ignoring her rudeness, Bea said, "Well, I spoke to your doctor, and we're going to fix that today."

"Yes, we're here to take you out for a spin," said Trinity, grinning.

"What on earth are you talking about?" muttered Lillian, turning her head to the wall, hoping that they would just leave.

"We OK'd it with your doctor, dear, and we're going to get you into a wheelchair and scoot you on down to see your husband. I know you want to see him, right?"

Lillian looked around at the sistahs and Pauline and asked suspiciously, "I don't get it. Why are you doing this?"

"Because we know you would do it for us if the tables were turned," said Dawn wickedly. The sistahs burst into laughter, and even Lillian joined in.

"We're doing it because it needs to be done, dear. Your doctor says that you can make the trip—that it would be good for you. And we're game, so let's go."

The four sistahs and Pauline helped Lillian out of her bed amid Lillian's rude insults and complaints and landed her gently in a wheelchair. Then off they went out the door, down the hall, into the elevator, and down to intensive care.

"We can't all go in, but we have clearance for one of us to go into the room with you, Lillian. You ready?" asked Bea, preparing to push Lillian into the room herself.

"In that case, I want *her* come with me." Surprisingly, she was pointing at Pauline.

"Me?" asked Pauline, no less astonished than anyone else.

"Yes, I trust you. Let's go," demanded Lillian, her head held high.

"OK, you got it, Miss Lillian." Pauline obliged with a big, toothy smile and pushed her into the room.

After they were gone, Dawn said, "What was that all about? I wonder why she wanted Pauline."

Bea answered, "The same reason women like to talk to her on the Friendship Bench. She's got a big heart, and they trust her with theirs. They believe that she cares—and she does. There's a lot more to our Pauline than pink hair and hot pants."

Pauline pushed Lillian's wheelchair to the side of Jack's bed. He was hooked up to tubes and machines that beeped, and he looked deeply asleep. Too deeply. Unconscious.

Lillian was able to lean over, somewhat painfully, and stroke his face gently. She took his hand in hers and whispered softly to her husband, "Jack, I'm here. I can't stay long, but I miss you and wanted to tell you that I'm alright and that you're going to be alright too. You take as much time as you need to sleep and heal, but then you come back to me, alright?"

Pauline watched as a single tear ran down Lillian's usually composed face, and she felt her own tears welling up. She couldn't help but reach out to put a comforting hand on Lillian's shoulders.

They stayed silent at the bedside for a few minutes, with Lillian simply holding onto her husband's hand and willing as much love as she could muster into the connection. Eventually, a nurse put her head into the room and said, "Mrs. Deslattes, the doctor wants you to go back to your room and rest now."

As Pauline readied the chair for the return trip, Lillian whispered to the prone man, "Sweetheart, I love you. Be on the lookout for me, OK? I'll call you again tonight."

When they returned Lillian to her room and got her settled back into her bed, she was utterly exhausted and on the verge of falling dead asleep. But before she went under, she once again pointed to Pauline and said, "You come back tomorrow."

The five women were stepping out of the hospital front door into the streaming sunlight when Pauline told them, "I'm glad they let Miss Lillian use the phone. I heard her tell her husband that she would call him again tonight. Not sure how that works, but it's real nice."

The sistahs looked at one another and nodded imperceptibly.

"The alcohol doesn't hurt either."
—Dawn

CHAPTER 33

During the days leading up to Lola's fundraising treasure hunt for the Safe House, employees and volunteers pitched in to make it a unique event. Lola decided to call it the Safe House Town-Wide Art Treasure Hunt, and participants were encouraged to wear pirate outfits for the hunt and at the night event as well. Lola knew that Louisianians love any reason to dress in costume, and a prize for the best pirate costume would be announced that evening.

The sistahs were right in the thick of all the work that needed to be done. Judith's two-dozen paintings needed to be delivered to those local businesses who paid to be event sponsors.

There was a flurry of last-minute ticket purchases, and the small city of Covington was abuzz with excitement. Everyone seemed to be involved, and it was the main topic of conversation all over town. Everyone hoped to be one of the twenty-four winners.

It was a very physically involved event which made it quite different from most fundraisers where people showed up at a gala, danced, ate, and threw money at a cause. Some events might include an auction, and some just asked for direct donations. At this event, they had to go out and find their own prizes.

On the Saturday morning of the hunt, all ticket holders received a treasure map of the town. There were twenty-four treasures hidden at twenty-four different businesses. Participants and ticket holders had to actively show up at the businesses and present their tickets to claim their treasures. One prize painting per ticket was allowed.

At nine o'clock on Saturday morning, the list of clues was emailed out to all the ticket holders, and the race was on. Any businesses that were not usually open at nine on Saturday mornings were sure to be on this particular day.

Signs were everywhere advertising the hunt. Anyone in the city who didn't know about the treasure hunt, and there weren't very many, who was just out for a coffee or a run, was startled and perplexed by the teams of pirates stalking the streets, conferring with their phones for clues, and shouting "Arrrgh!" at passing cars just for the fun of it. Even the dogs in the neighborhoods howled and barked their approval at passing pirates.

The local Times-Picayune headline ran a headline the next day:

Pirates Invade Covington

A story followed that described the event and included an account of an altercation that took place in St. John's Coffeehouse:

> **When the first two ticket-holding pirates showed up at St. John's Coffeehouse at the same time to claim a painting, the owner of the coffeehouse explained that the treasure hunt rules required them to toss a coin to determine the winner. One pirate, Wilma Hopkins of Covington, who was dressed in a ruffly, white shirt, eye patch, and and carried a plastic saber, said, "Nonsense. We're pirates, matey! We don't toss coins."**
>
> **Then she said to her competitor, Michael Bullington, also of Covington and who was also carrying a toy saber, "Aye matey, I challenge you to a duel! Winner takes all."**
>
> **Bullington accepted the challenge, and the two drew their sabers and danced back and forth**

between tables occupied by many coffee drinkers who cheered their favorite pirate.

When Hopkins accidentally knocked off one of Bullington's oversized buttons on his costume, tearing the sleeve slightly, she was immediately declared the winner by the cheering patrons. But she conceded the contest out of sheer guilt and offered to sew Bullington's button back on for him. Bullington went home with the prize painting by Judith Lafferty and Hopkins went home with the second-place prize—a print by the same artist which she claimed she "liked better anyway."

The winners and other guests gathered for the celebratory cocktail and hors d'oeuvres party at five o'clock that evening. A local band played, and the pirate-garbed guests danced under a crisscross of tiny lights, which turned the town trailhead, where the farmers market usually took place, into a festive sight.

"Oh my God, I can't believe how great everything turned out," said Lola, when the sistahs finally got a moment to sit and enjoy themselves along with the crowd. She happily raised a flute of champagne to clink with her friends.

"I think everyone is having such a good time," Judith said, watching couples dance by, sporting eye patches and pirate hats.

"Asking people to wear a bit of costume always brings out the fun in people," said Trinity, who had been in charge of outfitting this small group with pirate wear. She had come up with fluffy white shirts, eye patches, toy swords and daggers, and hats. Dawn even wore a fake mustache and a beard.

"The alcohol doesn't hurt either," Dawn laughed and scratched at her itchy facial hair. "Have you noticed that all these pirates started out yelling 'Aarrgh' nice and strong, but now, after cocktails, they are beginning to sound a little slurred." She let loose with a drunken version of the pirate's call, and the sistahs joined her, laughing.

"I think it was just a big win-win for everyone," said Lola. "The Safe House made a bunch of money, and Judith got a bunch of great exposure and got to clean up her house of old paintings. All the sponsors' businesses not only had great exposure too, but people actively had to come into their place of business for the treasure hunt. You know that's gotta help businesses out. Plus, the town gets to have a party. Now that's a win-win-win-win."

"Not to mention that we got to see Dawn in a mustache," said Helen, nudging her old friend.

"And Pauline is having the time of her life," said Trinity, nodding her chin towards the dance floor where Pauline led a group of women, probably her new Friendship Bench groupies, in a rather sexy rendition of the electric slide. She saw that Bitsy was talking to Pauline while the group danced. Trinity wondered what that was about but then she yelped, "Did I see a bit of twerking going on there?"

"Pauline never fails to surprise," laughed Judith.

At that point, Dawn leaned over and whispered to Lola, "Speaking of surprises, I have another one for you." She said it with a twinkle in her hazel eyes peeking over the itchy beard and mustache.

Lola groaned, then laughed. "I'm almost afraid to ask. OK, I'll bite. What is it?"

Dawn whispered again, and the whole table heard Lola's sudden gasp.

The other sistahs stared at her questioningly. Helen asked, "What's going on over there, you two?"

But Lola was too excited to answer. Instead, she asked, "Dawn, are you serious?"

Dawn nodded, and Lola lunged and threw her arms around her best friend. "You amaze me, sistah! Should we do this now?"

Dawn grinned, and Lola jumped to her feet. The two of them hurried up to the band and borrowed their microphone. Lola tested it with a tap, then said, "Hi everyone. I just have to interrupt for just a minute to tell you. The Safe House has just received the most miraculous news!"

The crowd quieted down and waited for Lola, who looked like she was going to burst with excitement. "I know many of you know her already—and it is a 'her' even though she looks pretty spiffy in facial hair and dressed like a swashbuckler."

The crowd chuckled, and Lola continued, "But for those of you who don't recognize her, I'd like to introduce Dawn Berard. Dawn is the CEO of Berard Accounting Firm and also the co-owner of the Gumbeaux Sistahs Gallery. I'm going to turn over the mic to her now because she has an announcement to make. Dawn . . ." She held the mic out to her friend.

Dawn stepped forward, saying, "You know, I could get used to this beard. Ladies, you know what I'm talking about. When I have a bad hair day, I put on a hat. But if I have a bad face day—and it happens—well, then I could put on this beard!"

She had everyone in the crowd laughing now, and the sistahs back at the table were cracking up.

"I do have some news for you tonight," Dawn continued. "As many of you know, my husband, Dan Berard, recently passed away. He and I had established a fund a few years ago with the idea that we would add to it occasionally. We wanted it to build up to a sizeable amount, and then we could donate it to a worthy cause. Well, tonight, we have our cause. So, in honor of my husband, I'd like to donate this check in the amount of thirty-thousand dollars to the Safe House."

Many gasps of surprise came from the crowd, and Dawn went on, "Both Dan and I always believed in the Safe House cause completely and have seen firsthand the difference it can make to the survivors of domestic violence. So tonight, we confirm our belief in their cause and hope that you will too."

Lola took back the mic, "Dawn, your gift will make a huge difference in what happens to those survivors. I know I speak for the Safe House in saying that we can't thank you enough." Lola took the check from Dawn and then threw her arms around her friend again to the music of the crowd cheering and clapping in a standing ovation.

The two women headed back to their table and were immediately surrounded by members of the Safe House board. They thanked Dawn sincerely. When they finally took their seats again, Bud had produced a couple more bottles of champagne for the table, and glasses were filled for their celebration. They toasted to both the success of the event and to Dawn's generosity.

"It really is a great success tonight," said Lola. She raised her glass and said loudly, "Let's toast to Judith's amazing idea for this whole fund-raising event and, of course, to Dawn and her magical checkbook!"

Helen raised her glass then, "And to Lola who put it all together. I know the board is thrilled with your efforts."

Bea smiled mischievously at Lola, "Yes dear, they will probably ask you to be in charge of fundraising next year, too, since you have such a talent for it."

Lola groaned, then chuckled, "Oh brother. There's a lesson here. Me and my big mouth."

Bud leaned over to his wife and whispered, "You are good at it. And if I didn't say it before, I'm really proud of you. You pulled it off."

Judith spoke up, "Actually, I was thinking about it, Lola. Now that my house is cleaned out of old paintings, I got worried about being able to repeat the event next year. But then I realized that Covington has a lot of artistic talent. It seems to attract southern artists. I'll bet there is another artist, or a group of artists, who would step up to the plate for the Safe House next year. Especially when I tell them that the Gumbeaux Sistahs Gallery has been swarming with customers since I got this exposure."

"It's true," said Dawn. "We've been swamped. Pauline has been helping out a bit, but I think we're going to need to hire someone."

"That's fabulous," said Trinity. "Your work has even been flying off the shelves faster in the New Orleans gallery too, Judith."

"I'll have to bring you some more. Oh wait, I'm cleaned out!" Judith said happily. She started to tell Trinity that she would get to work right away on some new paintings when she felt a hand touch her shoulder from behind.

"Hey there, Miss famous artist. How about a dance with a humble carpenter?"

She turned to find the gentle, brown eyes of Marty, and she stood to hug him. "Hey, Mister, how about a dance with an exhausted artist? You might have to hold me up, though."

Marty easily took her in his arms as they reached the dance floor, and a slow number was playing.

"You sistahs pulled it off again. I'm so proud of you," he whispered into her ear.

"Good Lord, I'm proud of all of us," she laughed. "It always amazes me what this group can accomplish. And by the way, I know I've said it before, but thanks for your help in getting this night together. Everybody pitched in so much, and it was so much work! But everybody's effort is appreciated."

"My pleasure," he said, smiling. "And speaking of my pleasure . . ." He held her away from him at arms-length and looked into her eyes.

Judith winced because she knew what he was going to say. She hadn't had five minutes to think about his proposal during the commotion of the event. She had promised herself that she would give it her total attention afterward.

"Oh dear," she said aloud.

"Oh dear?" said Marty, surprised. "Wait, that doesn't sound promising."

"Oh, Marty, I really don't want to do this tonight."

"Do what?"

"I really need to talk to you about something," she said.

Marty stopped dancing and looked at her seriously, "What is it? Just tell me."

"This doesn't exactly feel like the right time and place, but I guess I have no choice. It can't wait any longer."

"Judith, are you breaking up with me?" he asked quietly but bluntly.

"No! Oh no, Marty. That's not what this is at all. I love you way too much for that. Please don't think that!"

"Well, what then?" he asked, puzzled.

"OK then, here goes," she said with a sad sigh. "Marty, I need to give you your ring back. I just can't get married. Every time I think about it, I get panic attacks. Everything about it screams to me that it is a mistake."

Mary looked down at the floor, visibly upset. "Oh, I see."

"But I still want us to be together," she went on hurriedly, sick at the thought of losing him over this.

"I guess if you don't want to get married, then you shouldn't." He raised her hand and helped her remove the sparkly ring from her finger.

"Marty, I can tell you're upset," she said anxiously.

"Well, it's not exactly how I pictured this night going. You see, I had this fantasy that we could walk up to the microphone over there and make our big announcement."

Blushing and feeling terrible for him, she said, "Oh, actually, that would have been cool. I'm so sorry, Marty." She was suddenly completely exhausted.

"It's OK, Judith. It really is. Let's get you back to your seat. It's been a long night."

He returned her to her seat just as his assistant, Brenda, approached him and said, "Can I steal him away, Judith? Come dance with your assistant, Marty," she said coolly, smiling up at him.

"He's no father, step or otherwise."
—Cooper

CHAPTER 34

A few afternoons later, Helen opened her front door for Bea, and they immediately headed to the kitchen.

"Thanks for coming over, Bea. I seriously need your help here."

"Glad to, dear," said Bea sympathetically. "This is a tricky subject you're dealing with, and Coop always avoids it. That just makes everything harder. I'm not sure what his objection is, but I'm sure he doesn't want to hurt your feelings in any way."

"Well, I'm expecting him home any second because I made gumbo, and that boy will do most anything for gumbo. He's not a Gumbeaux Sistah, but he would make a perfect gumbreaux."

Bea giggled, "Yes, we have few gumbreauxs hanging around now—Bud, Marty, and now Coop."

"Well, my idea is that while he's here to eat, we have him as a captive audience. But he inhales his food, so we'd better talk fast."

Right on cue, Cooper lumbered into the side door, yelling in a fake deep voice and laughing, "Bring on the gumbo! There's a starving man here."

Both Helen and Bea hugged him and got him to sit down with them while Helen served the meal. Bea made him wait for a quick grace with folded hands. He obliged but kept one eye on the steaming bowl of dark-rouxed gumbo.

When he finally got a spoonful into his mouth, he laughed and said, "If you prayed that this gumbo would be heavenly, Miss Bea, then your prayers were answered. Man, I could eat this stuff every day for the rest of my ever-loving life."

Helen cut her eyes at Bea and said cautiously, "Well, Coop, speaking of the rest of your ever-loving life, there are things we need to talk about."

"I know. I'm excited about possibly getting into art school. I still owe them one more entrance test painting, and then we'll see. My fingers are crossed."

"I know. That would be so wonderful, dear. I pray about it for you every night. And about other things too,"

Cooper looked at her curiously, "Like what?"

Bea strove forward, "We've never discussed the situation with your stepfather and what will become of you. You need to deal with this, dear."

"That's right, Coop," interrupted Helen. She took a deep breath and surged forward, "We heard from my lawyer and the judge about your situation. Andre is back to jail for harassing you on the street, but he'll be out again soon enough. And because he's legally your father, he does still have some say in what happens to you, even though I'm your foster mother."

Cooper scowled darkly, "He's no father, step or otherwise." He shook his head, and Helen could see the pain in his eyes.

"He doesn't deserve you, Coop. There's something deeply wrong with him," said Bea. "I pray for him, but I admit I don't feel much like asking the Lord to heal him. I do it anyway because someone has to."

"I'd like to ask that he be dropped in a hole somewhere," said Helen fiercely.

Cooper laughed, "You sound like Miss Dawn now."

She grinned at him and went on, "The judge did make a suggestion, Coop."

Bea nodded encouragement at her, and so Helen said, "He said that if I adopted you formally, the legal ties with your father would be over. He said he would be willing to go that route, and he thinks it's the best thing for you."

"It will be over with anyway when I turn eighteen," said Coop.

"But that's not for a little while yet, Coop, and even after you're eighteen, he will still be your next of kin, which grants him certain legal rights. You need legal protection right now. Andre is out there and you're not safe. And you'll also need financial help," said Bea.

"Well, I've already promised to help him financially, best as I can, as he goes through school. Of course, I'm not wealthy by any means but I'll do my best," said Helen. "So that's not really the point. It's not the reason I want to adopt you, Coop."

Cooper looked at her, waiting with a sudden glimmer of fear in his eyes. "You don't have to make any promises to me, Miss Helen. People have promised things to me my whole life, and then they leave me, or worse, they beat the crap out of me."

Tears sprang into Helen's eyes, and she was surprised to see them in Cooper's eyes, as well. "I don't want to promise anything to you," she said. "I know how you feel about that. I want to adopt you because I want to be your family. I love you, Coop. I want to give you and me some people to call our own. You know, people who you can eat Christmas dinner with. Who can give you away when you marry Zoe. Who will hold your kids while they call me 'Nana.' I want a family, and I want to give you one too."

Helen's tears were streaming down her cheeks at this point, and she reached out for Cooper's hand. He held it tightly.

Then he said, his voice hoarse with emotion, "Miss Helen, you're killing me here. I have to admit that I never looked at families like that before. And I never realize that you needed a family too."

She whispered, "Yes. I need you, boy."

Suddenly he gave her a grin that brought pure sunshine, "OK, Miss Helen. Let's adopt each other."

Helen flew across the table to hug him while Bea looked on, overcome with happiness.

"Nicest thing that ever happened to me. Thank you, Miss Helen."

"Thank you too . . . son," choked Helen.

Then Cooper looked up at her slyly, "And don't think I didn't catch what you said about me marrying Zoe." He shook his head at her, grinning.

They all laughed this time, and Helen said, "Don't mind your old ma! She says the craziest things!" She turned and winked at Bea.

“I may just have to give your wife a run for her money.”
—Mrs. Albertson

CHAPTER 35

Lola stood back and gave her husband, Bud, the stink eye, hiding a smile at the same time.

She was in the main building of the Broussard's Nursery with Bud, Mrs. Albertson, and her daughter, Doris. They were all standing in front of a corner display of plants and garden tools where Mrs. Albertson had her arms wrapped tightly around Bud's torso. Lola could barely contain her laughter.

"Bud," said Mrs. Albertson, "I knew you were big and handsome, but now I know that you're good and kind, too. I may just have to give your wife a run for her money."

"Don't think she doesn't mean it, Lola," whispered Doris, chuckling.

Bud looked about as uncomfortable as a person could. He shot imploring looks at this wife, who ignored him for a while, then took pity on him. "Mrs. Alberton, you leave my husband alone." she demanded, laughing.

"Yes, mom, turn Bud loose, and let's get ready for your demonstration."

Reluctantly and somewhat sadly, Mrs. Albertson unwrapped herself from Bud's body.

"People will be here any minute for your class," said Bud, relieved.

That cheered the old woman up, "OK Bud, I can't wait to get started. For this month's class, I'm talking about propagating succulents. And I've brought a lot of my exotic plants so people can make cuttings. They're going to be thrilled. You can't get plants like this around here."

"Ooh, may I take a couple of cuttings too, Mrs. Albertson? I'd love to have some of these," asked Lola, fingering one of the plants.

"Only if you take my class," the old lady said coldly.

Lola shook her head, and Doris whispered to her, "I'll get you a couple, Lola. Don't worry. It's nothing personal. She just wants your husband." She winked at Lola mischievously.

Mrs. Albertson moved away from the group and started arranging her display corner, which now sported a sign that read, *Mrs. Albertson's Plant Demonstrations. See front counter for monthly schedule.*

Doris turned to Bud and Lola and said, "I can't thank you enough for allowing her to be queen bee here once a month. She's so excited—it's all she talks about. I mean it when I say you've added years to her life. We're both grateful to you."

"It's our pleasure, Doris. And our honor, really. Your mom knows more about plants than anyone we know. She really is the queen bee."

Doris lowered her voice and said, "And hopefully, these classes will bring you business and go towards making up for what she did. And maybe staying busy will help keep her thieving little fingers from cutting and stealing from you."

Even as she spoke, her mother produced her little silver scissors from a bag and snipped off a cutting from a nearby begonia.

Dan groaned, and Lola burst out laughing.

“Don’t make me laugh, my ribs are cracked, remember?”
—Lillian

CHAPTER 36

Pauline helped Lillian move her new walker down the hospital corridor to her husband's room. Pauline had taken to visiting Lillian every day for the past week to help her make this trek.

"Miss Lillian, you're getting to be a whiz with that walker. Pretty soon, you're gonna be racing me down the hall, and my money will be on you!" said Pauline, laughing loudly.

Lillian chuckled then groaned, "Pauline, don't make me laugh. My ribs are cracked, remember?" She scolded but smiled at the other woman at the same time. There was something about Pauline's kind heart and humor that brought out Lillian's affectionate side.

They reached Jack's room, and Lillian shuffled up to his bed. She felt her heart leap when she realized that his eyes were open, and he was staring up at her.

"Oh my god, Jack! You're awake," she cried and turned to Pauline. "Pauline, get the nurse!"

Pauline ran out of the room, and Lillian grabbed her husband's hand. "Jack, can you hear me?"

He answered very slowly but clearly, "Sure, I can hear you, Lillian."

Lillian felt tears rush to her eyes as she held her beloved husband's face. "Honey, I've missed you so much. It's so good to hear your voice. It's been so long."

At that, Jack looked a little more alert, saying, "What do you mean, Lillian honey? I just spoke with you on the phone last night."

Lillian gasped, and Pauline, who was standing in the doorway, started to pray.

"Miss Helen is no dummy."
—Cooper

CHAPTER 37

Dawn leaned over to whisper in Coop's ear so he could hear her above the revelry. "Well, I'd say this is one heck of a birthday present," she said. "You haven't even started school, and you already have an art gallery opening."

Cooper stood in front of the ten paintings he had included in the show and grinned at her. The gallery was crowded with cheerful art patrons. Cooper already had red dots by three of his paintings, indicating that they were sold.

"Oh my God, Coop," said Trinity hurrying over, "You're getting to be so successful. Promise me you'll do some pieces for the Royal Gala Art Gallery too by Christmas. Dawn and Judith aren't the only ones who love your work."

Coop grinned at them as he continued to answer questions for patrons. He happily explained his process and thoughts on the beautiful, large abstracts he had painted.

Bea watched him from across the room as she helped Helen give out champagne and bottled water at the coffee counter. She said quietly to Helen, "I don't think I've ever seen a happier young man. Ever."

"Or a happier older lady," answered Helen, beaming. "Speaking of which, I think it's time."

"Good luck, Helen," whispered Bea.

Helen went to the front of the room and stood up on a small footstool, using it as a podium. She grabbed a flute of champagne and took a deep breath, then she began hitting the side of her glass with a knife. The crowd looked up at the tinkling sound and quieted down.

"Friends, Gumbeaux Sistahs, and Gumbreauxs!" Helen said to a smattering of laughter. "This is a magical night for so many reasons. I'm so glad you're all here to share it with us. Cooper Landry is the man of the hour, so stand up, Coop, and let me talk about you a minute." She laughed, and Cooper stood, looking a bit bashful but smiling.

Helen went on, "I've got not one, but five bits of amazing, and like I said, magical pieces of news about Cooper. I almost don't know where to begin." She huffed and puffed exaggeratedly, pretending to be overwhelmed.

"First of all—Happy Birthday, Coop! That's right, how lucky to have your first art opening on your eighteenth birthday!"

Everyone clapped and shouted, "Happy Birthday!" to the young man, who smiled and waved, embarrassed by all the attention.

"And speaking of openings, Coop and I want to thank the Gumbeaux Sistahs Gallery for hosting this—his first art gallery opening."

Dawn hollered out, "We love you, Coop!"

Helen continued, "Dawn and Judith, as owners of the gallery, I think you have a winner on your hands. Not only is this his first show, but Coop just got word that he was accepted into the Loyola Art Department. He starts next fall!" The crowd clapped, and the sistahs all cheered and hollered for Coop.

"And for the fourth and fifth pieces of news, Coop, come on over here." He joined her, and she said, "Why don't you announce these?" She reached over and put her hand on his shoulder encouragingly.

Cooper cleared his throat and looked around. "Well, as Miss Helen said, it's my birthday, and today I turned eighteen. Many of you know that Miss Helen has been fostering me and that I didn't come from much of a family. Truth is, I had it pretty rough for a few years. Miss Helen took me in and helped me get my life straight. Shoot, she helped me get a life—period. I can't believe I'm here tonight with you all, and I can't believe I get to go to art school. I never dreamed this could happen. I owe a lot to her. Maybe some of you know that fostering ends when a kid reaches eighteen. After a foster kid reaches that milestone, they age out of the foster system. They are put out on their own just when they really need help transitioning to adulthood. Miss Helen is no dummy. She knows that. So, she and I talked, and then we went to see Judge Johnson."

At that, Coop indicated a tall gentleman in the corner and smiled. He went on, "We owe a lot to the judge, and I thank him for coming tonight. None of this would have happened without him. So, to make a long story short, Miss Helen and I have decided to become a family. We are officially adopting each other."

Gasps of surprise went up from the crowd, and many eyes well up with overwhelmed tears of happiness. Helen was no exception, and she spoke around her tears, "And as of yesterday, Coop has taken my last name. He is now Cooper Hoffmann."

"What?" yelled Dawn. Helen and Coop had kept that last part a secret. Not even the sistahs knew, so they surged forward and grabbed hold of Cooper, hugging him hard and then drawing Helen into the big group hug too.

He pulled away from them just long enough to say to the crowd, "One last thing. Miss Helen, thank you. I love you."

Helen covered her face with her hands and wept with happiness.

“I’m not marrying you!”
—Zoe

CHAPTER 38

The evening was drawing to a close, and the only people left were the sistahs and a few friends and family. Dawn chose that moment to drag a little stool to the center of the room. She stepped up while she dinged a knife against her wine glass.

The sistahs and their friends looked up in surprise. "What are you up to, Dawn?" called Lola.

"I have a little announcement of my own to make tonight," she said mysteriously.

Bea looked at Judith, "Do you know what this is about?"

Judith shrugged, "Not a clue." She added with a bit of a grin, "but it's Dawn. It could be literally anything."

Dawn looked like the cat that ate the cream up on her little makeshift podium as she said, "OK, so y'all know that Dan left that money in the fund for me to give to a worthy cause, right? I'm here to announce that I've picked that cause." She paused for reaction.

They all paused with her, confused. Then Lola broke the silence, "You've lost it, Dawn. You already gave the check to Safe House."

Dawn chuckled, "I knew this was going to be fun." Then she held up an envelope dramatically. "Well, I've decided that there was another cause that was so worthy that I had to write another check. This time it comes out of my own money."

"What! Good Lord, Dawn! That is so generous. What other cause did you choose?" asked Helen.

Dawn stepped down from the stool carefully and walked over to the group, holding out the envelope. She put it into Cooper's hands.

"Coop, honey, I want to contribute to your college fund. I can't think of another cause I love more than furthering your education and art career. I'm so proud of you and, as your auntie, it gives me a whole lot of happiness to do this. Will you please accept it?"

Cooper was stunned. He got to his feet with his mouth wide open in shock and disbelief. He stammered, "Holy cow. Are you serious, Miss Dawn?"

"I've never been more serious, Coop."

Cooper looked at Helen, who nodded with tears in her eyes. She mouthed the words "thank you" to her sistah and found herself overcome with emotion.

"Auntie Dawn," Coop said with a big grin, "I can't accept fast enough! And I can't thank you nearly enough, too. This will make such a big difference—to me and to Miss Helen, I mean my mom." He started to lean over and kiss Dawn's cheek, but Dawn captured him in a giant bear hug instead.

The sistahs cried out joyfully and surrounded the two of them.

"Congratulations, Coop!"

"We're so happy for you!"

"Dawn, you're amazing!"

While Dawn still had a hold on Cooper, she whispered, "Welcome to the family, Coop. And, by the way, you should know that you have Zoe to thank for this too. It was her idea to give you the money, and it was a wonderful one. It's been so hard to keep it a secret from everyone. I just can't believe I didn't tell the sistahs, but I'm glad I didn't. It was fun shocking the hell out of them." she chuckled.

Later as the gallery was clearing out, Zoe made her way across the main room to Cooper's side. "Well, I don't know what to congratulate you on first. There's so much going on in your life. You are really coming into your own, Cooper Landry, I mean Hoffmann."

"Thanks," he said, looking up at the girl with freckles and pretty, blue eyes. "I hear congratulations are in order for you too."

She cocked her head questioningly, so he went on, "I understand you are joining forces with my Aunt Lola and going into the landscaping business. And that you've decided what to major in finally."

"Word gets around," smiled Zoe.

"With this group? You bet it does," he laughed. "I don't think you could do better than to hook up with the Gumbeaux Sistahs."

"You either," she said, "And now we're both related to one of them. We're probably distant cousins at this point." They both laughed, and then Zoe said softly, "You know, Coop, I can't help but think that we got off on the wrong foot—that we misjudged each other. Do you agree?"

"Yes, we did. I blame you for that," he said.

"Ditto," she said, chuckling. "But I'm glad you're finally coming around and can see the error of your ways."

"Ditto," he said back to her, smiling.

Their eyes met, and Zoe felt something warm up in her heart—something small but definitely there. Her cheeks flushed, and it made him smile even broader.

His expression suddenly turned serious. "Listen, I want to say thanks. I hear it was your idea for Aunt Dawn to give me the college fund."

Zoe blushed and looked at her feet, "Oh shoot. Mamere has a big mouth. She wasn't supposed to tell."

"Oh well, it's a pretty big secret. I guess she had to tell someone. I'm glad it was me. That was a really nice thing to do." He grinned at her, "One might think that you actually like me." Then his eyes crinkled in the corners with merriment. "You do know, Zoe, that your grandmother and our aunties are conspiring for us to marry someday," he said bluntly and watched her reaction with a mischievous grin.

Zoe snorted and said, laughing, "You wish! Besides, we're related now."

"We're not that related," he replied.

She took that cue to head towards the front door, saying with a coy smile, "Happy Birthday, Cooper Hoffmann."

"Goodnight, Zoe Abadie," he smiled back.

As the door closed behind her, he heard her yell loudly, "I'm not marrying you!"

He chuckled and looked across the room right at that moment, only to find the sistahs grinning delightedly at him from behind the cash register. He covered his eyes with his hands and groaned.

"You bet your ass I will!"
—Pauline

CHAPTER 39

Lillian and Pauline sat next to Jack's bed in the hospital, and Pauline helped him by spooning Jello into his mouth. He was still a bit shaky and weak, so she helped him with meals.

"You're too good to me, Pauline," he mumbled around the sweet dessert.

"Well, y'all are good people who have had some bad breaks," said Pauline. "And Lord, I know how that is. And I like helping out."

He laughed and said, "Yes, in fact, we literally had some bad breaks," glancing at the cast on Lillian's leg as she smiled up at him.

Then she turned to Pauline, "Listen, Pauline, Jack and I have been talking. We're both going to need some help when we go home in a few days. We were wondering if you'd like to work for us as our caregiver in our house. You're so good at it, and neither of us wants anyone else in our home."

"What?" yelped Pauline. "If that ain't the craziest idea! Miss Lillian, you know I'm not qualified for that. The only thing I'm qualified for—and I mean I could give lessons in it—is how to be a broke-ass streetwalker."

Even uptight Lillian had to laugh at that one. "Oh, I think you are delightful, Pauline. But you don't have to worry about all that. I've given this a lot of thought, and here's what I propose. You can live with Jack and me in our home. We'll pay all your expenses and help you get into a local caregiver certification class, which we'll pay for also."

"You have got to be kidding!" shouted Pauline. "I've had nothing but bad breaks all my life, and now, suddenly, I get the best break ever?"

"You've been a good break for us too, Pauline. You've made a big difference to both of us. Besides, you keep us laughing all the time, which is good medicine, as they say."

"You keep me laughing too, Miss Lillian, although, I don't think you mean to," teased Pauline.

Lillian burst out laughing, "You see! You're wickedly funny!"

"Please say you'll do it, Pauline. Lillian and I need you," pleaded Jack

Pauline looked from one to the other and said thoughtfully, "Hmm, I have one condition."

Jack and Lillian looked at each other, surprised and not knowing what to expect. "What is it?" they asked.

"I'm hoping that you'll both consider letting me dye your hair to match mine. Pink is all the rage, and can you just imagine how heads would turn when I took you to your doctor appointments?"

Jack swallowed hard, but Lillian just laughed loudly, "What if I say we'll consider it, Pauline?"

Pauline slapped her hands to her thighs and stood up laughing, "Ok then, yes! You bet your ass I will!"

Lillian actually clapped, and Jack said, "Thanks so much, Pauline."

"This is great in so many ways. I will work hard for you folks and take good care of you. And it will also help get a new career. I mean, I like counseling on the Friendship Bench, but there's not a lot of money in it." She laughed, then she grew serious, "And if Benny gets a mind to come looking for me again, he'll never think to look for me at your house. It's one more step away from that old life of mine." Then Pauline put her hand one over her mouth and said, "Oh wait a minute. It'll break Miss Judith's heart if I leave her."

"Something tells me she'll be happy for you, Pauline," said Lillian, grinning.

"There's not a bit of her that's real."
—Judith

CHAPTER 40

"Pauline just told me she's moving in with Lillian, of all people," Judith told Marty as they sipped coffee on his back porch. Judith had brought over some homemade scones that morning, and now Marty helped himself.

"Oh my, these are amazing!" he said, his eyes rolling with delight.

"Well, they're special. I added my mom's recipe for lemon glaze on them. They're a hit every time I find the time to make them and bring them to the gallery."

"Whatever you do, don't tell me when you deliver. Otherwise, I'll go buy every one of them—every time." He laughed and took another bite. "I could eat these all day."

She smiled, watching him enjoy her cooking. His sweet nature and crazy sense of humor were the best combinations she could ask for in a man. And for bonus points, he was cute too. His warm, brown eyes crinkled in the corners with a smile. He caught her looking at him and told her, "You're a remarkable woman, Judith Lafferty."

She grinned. "Thank you, Marty. You're pretty remarkable yourself."

He leaned towards her and spoke softly, "There's no way on earth I could help but fall in love with you."

She flushed but didn't look away from him. "I love you a ridiculous amount too, Marty."

Then he glanced nervously around, first up then down, then stared at his feet. He was obviously worried about something. "You know, we never did finish our conversation."

"What conversation was that?" she asked him, but of course, she knew.

"If you don't remember, let me remind you by asking you once again—Judith, will you marry me?" he asked bluntly but lovingly.

"Marty," she answered slowly, "I thought we settled this. But listen, I have a question for you too."

He raised an eyebrow, and she went on, "If I say no to your proposal, is it a deal-breaker?"

He looked alarmed, so she hurried on, "Look, I love you. You know that. And you love me. I promise never to leave you and to love you until the day I die if you can do the same. But marriage and I don't get along. Apparently, I'm not good at it, and I've proven it over and over, Marty."

"That's just because you hadn't met the right man—till now."

"That may be. But I'm not willing to gamble your heart and mine on it. Especially since what we have is perfect. It's simply perfect. Let's not mess it up." She hesitated with a worried look in her eyes, "I'm just concerned that you have your heart so set on marriage that you'll run off with that assistant of yours. By the way, I hear tell that she has fake boobs and fake other stuff too—fake kidneys, fake muscles, fake brains—there's not a bit of her that's real. She's . . ."

Marty burst out laughing, "Stop! Stop! I get the picture! You're a crazy woman, in case I hadn't mentioned that before."

Judith laughed till she had tears in her eyes. "Sorry, that's not very nice of me, but I would definitely fight dirty for you, Marty. And I have to admit that I don't think I trust that woman around you. I didn't want to say anything about it in case I was wrong because I know she's a lot of help to you. But, sheesh, what a flirt! Think about it—if a cute, younger hunk was coming on to me, you'd be upset too.

You might even take a poke at him which is what I'd sometimes like to do to your assistant."

"Real or fake, you have nothing to worry about there. Brenda's been a real help to me. Not only does she help around the shop, but she also organizes all the shows I do selling my furniture. It saves me hours of work."

"Yeah, yeah. I know. She's perfect. I got that message already."

"But here's what you don't know, Judith. And you don't know because I thought I should keep it private for Brenda's sake, but I think I have to say something about it now for our sake. The thing is—Lola introduced me to Brenda."

"She did?" asked Judith, surprised.

"Yes, you see, with Lola's connection to the Safe House, she knew about Brenda. She knew that Brenda needed help and she thought of me and my new woodworking business. But Lola is not allowed to discuss any of the Safe House clients with people. That's why she didn't tell any of the sistahs. But just like Helen, Brenda was the victim of domestic abuse. She had to stay at the Safe House for a while trying to get her life back. I agreed to give Brenda a part-time assistant's job, and I helped her find a place to live too. She has a young daughter who's only nine, and the two of them have had a terrible time of it. And, OK, I know what you mean about Brenda being a little flirty—and that she's somewhat attractive. But it means nothing as far as I'm concerned. It's just her way, and I will speak to her about it if it makes you feel better. Maybe you'll be happy to know that she's got herself a new boyfriend—a good guy too. I happen to have introduced them. But, Judith, you have to believe me when I say that you are the only one I want. Just you."

She looked at him steadily, her heart swelling and knew that an important moment had arrived. She felt it in her bones. She suddenly jumped up from her chair and knelt down next to him. "Marty LeBlanc, I love you with all my heart, and I promise to be good to you and take care of you too. I want us to be lovers and fiancées, or whatever you want to call it. But I want you to live in your house, and I want to live in mine." She waited for what he would say, hope in her eyes.

"Well, let's see. How about this—will you wear the ring I bought for you?" He reached into his pocket and produced the beautiful square diamond solitaire he had given her before.

"Oh my!" said Judith. "Really? You don't have to. I wasn't expecting that." Then she changed her tune slightly, "Marty, it's so beautiful. Are you sure?"

"I've never been surer. I want you for my fiancée. Besides, introducing you as my lover just sounds stupid, don't you think?"

Judith grinned. Still kneeling, she asked, "Marty, I would love to be your fiancée if you promise to never, never, never marry me."

He chuckled as he put the ring on her finger. "I promise not to marry you for now. But I'll probably ask you again every few years. That work for you?"

"Fair enough," she said and leaned in to kiss her sweet man as hard as she could.

"Yes, you are chopped liver."
—Dawn

CHAPTER 41

Dawn was a few minutes late to Lola's place to meet the sistahs. When she arrived, Lola opened the door for her and then held out her open palm.

"What's this?" asked Dawn, looking into Lola's empty hand.

"I'm waiting for my thirty-thousand dollars too. If you're going to keep writing checks and handing out money, I want to be next in line. I mean, what am I, chopped liver?"

"Yes, you are chopped liver," said Dawn drolly, then slapped her friend's hand away with a laugh. "I'm starving, girl. I'm so ready for the world's second-best gumbo. Bring it on!" She chuckled and brushed past her friend.

"Second best, my eye," laughed Lola. "As always, and forever, my mom's gumbo is better than your mom's gumbo."

"Well, I'm willing to let you try and prove it. Let's eat!"

As the gumbo simmered, the sistahs enjoyed glasses of white wine and caught up with their usual loving, teasing banter. When the food was ready, the sistahs gathered around Lola's big wooden kitchen table. Plants lined the room on shelves and in hanging pots. Lola's kitchen always felt like a forest of blooming, healthy plants—a forest with amazing aromas coming from her old six-burner stove. She dished up big, steaming bowls of her gumbo and rice to Bitsy, Pauline, and the rest of the sistahs.

As she filled everyone's glasses with iced tea, Pauline said excitedly, "Can you believe it? Miss Lillian and Mr. Jack invited me to live with them as a caregiver, and they're gonna pay for my classes and certification too."

"That's just amazing," said Dawn. "And so of them nice too. Come to think of it, are you sure it was Lillian?"

Lola snickered and elbowed Dawn while Bea said, "OK dear, let's not jump on Lillian while she is doing something good for our friend." Then to Pauline, she said, "I'm glad we could get together today to celebrate your success, Pauline."

"Just think, I don't have to walk the streets no more, and Benny can just kiss my—"

Bea interrupted, "It's an amazing opportunity for you, Pauline. A real gift."

Then Bitsy said, "Pauline and I have been talking things over. We've decided that once her caregiving job at Lillian's is finished, Pauline will need a place to stay. I've been thinking of getting a roommate so it looks like Pauline will be moving in with me."

"It's the best idea! I can't wait for all this to happen, Miss Bitsy," enthused Pauline.

Bitsy cut her off, "OK but the deal's off if you keep calling me 'Miss!'"

"Oh right, I'll get it right one of these days," laughed Pauline. "Of course, with all these new developments in my life, I'll have to give up my post at the Friendship Bench. I won't have time for it now."

Bea and Helen gave each other a quick look of surprise and vast relief. This solved their problem of having to prevent Pauline from giving out felonious advice to her friendship bench groupies. Helen smiled and hurried to say, "Yes, but of course, you'll come and visit the gallery and all of us from time to time, won't you?"

"Couldn't keep me away," said Pauline, happily munching on a piece of French bread spread thickly with butter. "Besides, I was thinking that Miss Lillian should let me bring her phone back to you, Miss Dawn. She doesn't need it anymore now that Mr. Jack woke up."

"She can keep it," said Dawn. "It's OK."

"Oh no," said Pauline earnestly, "Someone else needs to have it now. After all, it worked so well for her and Mr. Jack."

Dawn stopped spooning gumbo into her mouth. "What do you mean, Pauline?"

"Really? Don't you know?"

"Know what?" asked Lola.

"While Mr. Jack was in his coma sleep, Miss Lillian talked to him every night on that phone. She always told me about it the next day when I came to visit her."

The sistahs looked at each other. Dawn put her spoon down and said slowly, "You mean she pretended to talk to him, right? She didn't really talk to him."

"Oh no, Miss Dawn. It was a genuine miracle. Miss Lillian called it uncanny. She had been worried about when the time came to leave the hospital to go home because she lost her house keys in the accident. She knew there was a spare key hidden outside of the house somewhere but couldn't remember where Mr. Jack had hidden it. She even told Mr. Jack on the phone one night that the key was missing. Miss Lillian often mentioned to me that she thought she could feel Mr. Jack's presence on the phone. One night she even thought she heard him breathing, and another night she was convinced that she heard a whisper come through the receiver. But this particular night, she told Mr. Jack how worried she was about the key and then she got off the phone and went to sleep. The next morning she woke up and knew right away that the key was hidden in a loose brick in the fence in their side yard. Miss Lillian said it was a sign from Mr. Jack. He was still looking out for her from wherever he was. Mr. Jack doesn't remember anything from when he was in the coma, but it doesn't matter. We know. No, Miss Dawn. No one is pretending about that phone. Miss Lillian and I true believers.

"Oh my Lord, Pauline!" said Dawn. "Are you sure?"

"I'm sure, and so is Miss Lillian. She wants to share the phone with other folks who might need to talk to their people who are not around anymore. I've been telling some of the women that sit with me on the Friendship Bench too."

Dawn gasped, and there were tears suddenly in her eyes. "Oh my heavens! There were times when I thought I heard Dan's voice while I was on that phone, but I didn't really believe it till just now."

"Miss Lillian said you have to be real quiet and hold real still. Of course, that's all she could do in that hospital bed."

"Pauline," said Dawn excitedly, "We have to get that phone back. Will you go to Lillian's house with me right after lunch?"

"Sure. I'll have to get back to my caregiving duties right afterwards anyway, Miss Lillian and Mr. Jack will be expecting me back home."

The sistahs finished up lunch, and Dawn was in a hurry to get to Lillian's house. But before she could get out of the door, Judith said, "Before you go, I want to show y'all something."

"What is it, dear?" asked Bea.

Judith held out her left hand dramatically, waving it around slowly back and forth.

"Oh my heavens above!" yelled Dawn. "Marty came through! You've been holding out on us, Judith. You're engaged again! When were you going to announce this?"

"I'm announcing it now, partner, and my announcement is this—Marty and I are officially not getting married."

Lola, who was all set to do a victory yell, stopped and said, "Wait what? You're not getting married?"

Dawn laughed, saying, "And you still got the ring? Way to go, Judith!"

"What exactly do you mean, dear?" asked Bea. "I think we need more information."

"Well, y'all know how I feel about marriage. But the truth is, Marty and I are crazy about each other. So, we promised to be affianced for the rest of our lives," she chirped happily.

Stunned, Dawn missed a beat, searching her partner's face for signs of insanity, or happiness. Finally, she said, "Well, why not? Congrats on not getting married, sistah!"

The girls raised what was left of the iced tea in their glasses and toasted, "To Judith and Marty. May they live happily, and separately, ever after."

They laughed, and then Dawn remembered that important errand that needed to be done immediately. She grabbed Pauline's arm, and said, "Let's go, Pauline. We've got a phone to collect."

“I’m a believer.”

—Dawn

CHAPTER 42

Two months later, the sistahs, along with Lillian, her husband Jack, Cooper, and Pauline, all stood in front of the Gumbeaux Sistahs Gallery in the early evening. Judith popped open a bottle of champagne and poured everyone a glass.

Dawn breezed up to the front stoop, lifted her glass, and toasted loudly, "Let's raise our glasses and christen this beautiful donation by Lillian and Jack." She pointed to a small, new, red structure in the corner of the gallery. "Lillian, I don't know where you came up with this old-time contraption, but it's perfect. I mean, where does one go to buy a telephone booth? And Coop, thank you for the beautiful sign you painted for it."

The colorful sign hung over the telephone booth and read *Spirit Phone.* The glass walls had been painted bright red and yellow in the interior so that people could have privacy.

"It even still has the old-fashioned, drop-coin phone inside."

"Thanks for your contribution too, Dawn," added Judith. "I know you split the expenses with the Deslattes."

"What can I say? I'm a believer," said Dawn.

"How will people know what it does?" asked Pauline. "People might just stop in and drop a nickel to call someone like a regular payphone, and it's not hooked up to anything."

"We're just gonna play it just like we did the Friendship Bench. Word of mouth will get it to the right ears."

"I hope they find the same comfort in it that it gave to me. It's a different phone, of course, but the idea is the same. They can drop by and call their missing loved ones and hopefully get some comfort from it," explained Dawn.

"Yes, comfort—and maybe more," said Lillian, quietly, looking at her husband with a deep prayer of thanks.

Judith headed towards the front door, "Y'all come on in and have some scones and coffee. Christening gives me an appetite."They trooped inside, and Judith told Lillian, "Isn't it amazing that all this hardship brought you and Pauline together."

"I can't believe how lucky we are to have her," said Lillian, thoughtfully. "If I've learned one thing this year, it's that there is a lot of magic in this beautiful world of ours. Shoot, just the fact that the sistahs and I are now actual friends is proof enough of that," she laughed.

"You might call that magic," laughed Dawn. "But I think it's more of a miracle."

"There's been a lot of miracles around here lately, and Jack and I want to say thank you for ours, Dawn. Thank you for the phone and for your compassion towards us. If it hadn't been for you, I'm not even sure that Jack would have made it. Talking to him every day made a big difference. Not only in his recovery but in our marriage as well. Since the accident, we both have come to realize how short life is, and how precious. We've talked it over in-depth, and for the first time, I believe that there is real forgiveness here and a chance for a new start. The truth is, I'm as happy with him, broken bones and all, as I've ever been. And Jack says he feels the same way."

Dawn reached out to Lillian, and the two ex-enemies, now newly found friends hugged with tears in their eyes.

Bea and Helen stood on the side and nodded their approval.

Lola, aware of the shift in circumstances, couldn't help but tease, "Hey, if we're all suddenly going to start being besties now, someone has to clue me in."

Pauline added, "Miss Lillian is one big love bug these days!"

"That I am," said Lillian happily, then helped herself with a newfound appetite to one of Helen's tempting golden-brown pastries.

A short time later, when they were all full of Helen's scones, they all filed back out of the front door and stopped in surprise. Three women and a man stood in line outside the Spirit Phone booth, waiting their turn.

"Now, how did that happen so quickly?" asked Helen.

Lola laughed and said, "Looks like that word of mouth you were talking about is more of a 'word of Big Mouth.'"

"It's a blessing, dears," said Bea. "Just as you all are." The group nodded their agreement and grinned affectionately at each other.

Then Dawn said, "Listen, I gotta go. I'm expecting an important call."

"Give 'em hell, Dawn, like you always do."
—Dan

CHAPTER 43

When Dawn arrived home, she settled deep into her den's comfy sofa with a glass of red wine. She took a few sips and prepared herself emotionally. When she felt ready, she reached out to the phone sitting next to her on the couch.

Lifting the receiver, she listened, half-expecting a dial tone, but of course, there was none. Then she dialed "1" on the rotary dial and waited for a sound of any kind, but all she could hear was her own breathing.

She whispered, "Dan?" Still, no sounds came from the phone, so she went on. "Honey, it's me. I just wanted to check in with you tonight and tell you what's been happening. I know you love gossip as much as I do." She relaxed into the couch more and went on, "So, thanks to Bea and Helen introducing Pauline to Lillian, she now lives and works for the Deslattes as a caregiver and is attending classes. She'll get her official certificate before too long. I can't believe how well that worked out for everyone. Can you believe it?"

She listened for any sign of a response. Not hearing any, she sighed and continued, "Coop got officially adopted by Helen. They are so happy, Dan. And he had his first art show at the gallery, and he's going to go to art school. Also, he's in love with Zoe, but he doesn't know it yet. As you know, men can be a bit slow about that kind of thing. And by the way, I think she likes him too."

"And Judith and Marty got engaged, sort of. I told her she was smart. She got the ring but didn't get hitched!" She laughed into the phone and felt a bit of warmth in her heart, almost as if she wasn't laughing alone.

"The gallery is doing well, and so is our accounting firm, so you don't have to worry about that." She hesitated, thinking.

"And you'll be happy to hear that I chipped in with Lillian and Jack, and we installed a Spirit Phone in front of the gallery. And boy, is it popular! I think it just makes people who have lost someone feel better. Well, I know it does."

Dawn closed her eyes as hot tears slowly filled them. "I'm going to keep calling, Dan. It's the only thing, aside from being with those crazy sistahs of mine, that makes me feel better. It's still so hard, honey. It's so hard." She swallowed as a tear ran down her cheek. "But I'm keeping busy. I just want you to know that I'm always thinking of you. I love you, Dan. And I always will."

She sat silently for a moment, then said, "Well, I guess that's it for now. I'll call again soon. Goodnight, honey."

She placed the receiver back on the phone cradle and sat there with her eyes closed, breathing slowly and feeling peaceful for the first time all week.

Dan still held the receiver of his Spirit Phone up to his ear and heard Dawn telling him the goings-on of her life without him. The sound of her voice was sweet music coming over the phone, and a calm smile shone on his peaceful face. While she spoke, he whispered to her, "Dawn, honey. I know you're sad, but I just wanted you to know that I'm fine here, and you're gonna be fine too. I'm so proud of the way you just keep going. I thank God every day for your strength and for the amazing friendships you have with the sistahs. I miss you, but I know I'll see you again someday. No hurry, though. Life still has a lot of magic to show you yet. Just know that the day you walk through those shiny gates, I'll be there with the biggest smile on my face you've ever seen."

"By the way, I'm so proud of the way you handled the charity fund gift. I would never have thought to give it to young Cooper, but I agree completely with your choice. Of course, I never would have thought to give an equal amount to the Safe House. You always did like to throw money around. I hope there's still some left!" he chuckled heartily. "Just kidding, honey. I know we're good for it. But I'm so relieved that I didn't leave you a million dollars to give away. No telling what you would have done!

"Meanwhile, give 'em hell, Dawn, like you always do. And know that I am wishing you a peaceful, gentle night, my love. Goodnight, my girl."

He set the phone down next to him but did not disconnect it. And he never would.

The End

GUMBEAUX SISTAH RECIPES

Funeral Potatoes

1 stick salted butter
1 medium onion, diced
1 30oz bag of frozen, shredded hash brown potatoes
¼ cup all-purpose flour
1 cup milk
2 cups chicken broth
Salt and ground pepper to taste
1-1/2 cups grated Monterey Jack cheese
1 cup sour cream
½ cup grated sharp cheddar cheese
2 cups kettle-cooked potato chips
¼ cup grated parmesan cheese

Preheat oven to 350 degrees. Grease a 9x13" baking dish with 1 tbs butter. Take the potatoes out of the freezer while you are preparing the rest of the ingredients.

Heat a large, deep skillet over medium-high heat, then melt 6 tbs of butter in it. Add the onions and cook, stirring occasionally, until the onions start to soften—about 3-4 minutes. Sprinkle the flour over the onions and stir to incorporate. Cook for 1-2 minutes, stirring occasionally—do not let flour darken. Whisk in the milk, making sure to get out all the lumps. Add the broth and whisk again if there are still lumps. Bring the mixture to a simmer and allow it to thicken— about 3 minutes. Season to taste with salt and pepper. Turn off the heat and stir in the Monterey Jack, sour cream and cheddar. Add the hash brown potatoes and mix everything together. Transfer the mixture to the prepared baking dish.

Melt the remaining 1 tbs butter in a small pan. Put the potato chips and parmesan in a bowl and crush the potato chips. Pour in the melted butter and toss to coat. Sprinkle the crumbs over the top of the potatoes.

Cover with foil and bake for 20 minutes, then remove the foil and continue baking until golden brown on top and bubbling around the edges, about 15 minutes more. Let rest for 15 minutes before serving.

Note: you can freeze this dish, but it is recommended that you do not add the potato chip topping until thawed and ready to serve.

Crawfish Monica (Lola's rendition)

A delicious, creamy pasta dish with a tiny kick!

1 lb. crawfish tails, preferably from Louisiana, boiled and peeled
1 stick butter
1 pint half-and-half
1-2 tbs garlic, chopped (to your taste)
1 bunch green onions, chopped
(save out 3 tbs and put aside for garnish)
1-2 tbs Creole Seasoning of your choice
1 lb cooked Rotelli or Fettuccini pasta
¾ cup freshly grated Parmesan cheese

Cook pasta according to the directions on the package. Drain. Save a tbs of the water in which the pasta was cooked. Melt the butter in a large pot and sauté onions and garlic for 3 minutes. Add the crawfish tails and sauté for 2 minutes. Add the half-and-half, then several big pinches of Creole seasoning, to taste. Cook for 5-10 minutes over medium heat until the sauce is bubbly and thickens. Add the 1tbs pasta water. Add it all to the pasta and toss well. Then add the cheese, toss again. Let it sit for 10 minutes or so over very low heat, stirring often. Serve immediately with green onion garnish—great with hot French bread and butter. Serves 4-6

Judith's Scones with her Mom's Special Lemon Glaze

2 cups all-purpose flour
1/3 cup sugar
1 tsp baking powder
¼ tsp baking soda
½ tsp salt
8 tbsp unsalted butter, frozen
1/2 cup sour cream
1 large egg

Adjust oven rack to lower-middle position and preheat oven to 400 degrees.

In a medium bowl, mix flour, sugar (reserve 1tsp of the sugar), baking powder, baking soda and salt. Grate butter into flour mixture on the large holes of a box grater. Use your fingers to work in butter (mixture should resemble coarse meal.)

In a small bowl, whisk sour cream and egg until smooth

Using a fork, stir sour cream mixture into flour mixture until large dough clumps form. Use your hands to press the dough against the bowl into a ball. (The dough will be sticky in places, and there may not seem to be enough liquid at first, but as you press, the dough will come together.)

Place on a lightly floured surface and pat into a 7-8 inch circle about ¾ inch thick. Sprinkle with remaining 1 tsp of sugar. Use a sharp knife to cut into 8 triangles; place on a cookie sheet (preferably lined with parchment paper), about 1 inch apart. Bake until golden, about 15-17 minutes. Cool for 5 minutes and serve warm or at room temperature. Makes 8 scones.

Special Note: for variety, you can add a generous tsp of finely grated orange zest to the dry ingredients and/or add ½ cup raisins or dried cranberries to the dough.

Mom's Lemon Glaze:

1 cup confectioners' sugar
1-1/2 - 2 tbsp fresh lemon juice
½ tsp lemon zest

In a small bowl, combine confectioners' sugar and lemon zest. Add in lemon juice until desired consistency is reached. Stir till smooth. Drop by spoonful over cooled scones and let it drip down the sides. Serve and enjoy.

Helen's Homemade Tomato Soup

4 tbsp olive oil
1 large onion, diced
1 cup carrots, thinly sliced
2 lbs fresh tomatoes
1 cup water plus 2 bouillon cubes (chicken or veggie)
2 tbsp honey or sugar
1 tsp salt, (or more to taste)
½ tsp pepper
10-15 basil leaves
Pinch of cayenne
½ cup Cream or half-and-half
1-2 tbsp sour cream (optional)

Garnish suggestions: extra chopped tomatoes for texture, basil pieces, croutons, grated fresh parmesan or pecorino cheese

Heat butter in a heavy-bottom pan over medium-high heat. Add the onion and sauté until softened—about 3-4 minutes. Add the carrots, lower heat to medium, sauté 3-4 minutes more until onions are golden and fragrant.

Add the tomatoes, water, bouillon cubes, honey or sugar, salt, and pepper. Stir, increase heat and bring to a simmer, cover, then lower heat to low, so it's gently simmering. Simmer 10-15 minutes until the tomatoes have broken down and carrots are tender. Remove from heat. Using an immersion blender, blend the soup, adding the basil leaves—or you can blend in a blender.

Return it to the pot and stir in the cream. Taste and adjust salt and sugar. Add little pinch of cayenne. Whisk in sour cream, if desired.

Serve in bowls with garnish. Enjoy!

ACKNOWLEDGMENTS

First off, I want to say thanks to all the readers, friends, and family who seem to love the Gumbeaux Sistahs as much as their author does. Your encouragement is like crack cocaine to me, and new GS adventures would not be happening without your enthusiasm. I feel we are all in this together, and the reviews you post on Amazon—well, you wouldn't believe how much those can help an author. Thank you, thank you, thank you!

I also want to thank Elizabeth Frey, my unrelenting and adored editor. Also, many thanks go to Ginny Hoffmann, Pemmie Sheasby, and Dian Lusher for being advance readers and sussing out the plot holes, weak spots, and nonsense that can show up at any given moment.

FYI: I recently discovered something about me and my writing. The first quarter of this book was written in my car parked under trees in the shade during the Covid quarantine. I had to get out of the house to write, and the car was the only place that felt safe to me. The other three-quarters of the book were written months later when the quarantine was eased, and I got the vaccine. Then I could haunt my favorite coffeehouse again. The big lesson here was—things don't work without coffee. Remember that!

You may have noticed that my book titles all begin with the word Gumbeaux, i.e., *Gumbeaux Sistahs, Gumbeaux Love,* and now, *Gumbeaux Magic.* It was recently suggested to me by the Rock 'n Readers Book Club that the next book should be entitled *Gumbeaux*

Sex. I laughed so hard when they told me that, I swear I was crying. I can't imagine what that would look like. Well, I can but I don't want to. Just to be sure, I asked several Gumbeaux Sistahs about their sex lives and each and every one of them told me to mind my own business.

Finally, I just want you to know that I continue to have great affection for you all as we go on this grand adventure together.

Gumbeaux on down, sistahs!

Jax

ABOUT THE AUTHOR

Jax Frey

Born in New Orleans, Jax Frey came into this world with a sense of celebration of Louisiana culture, food, family, and fun. Translating that celebration into her writing and onto canvas is her true calling. Her colorful art depicts everything Louisiana from her dancing *Gumbeaux Sistahs* paintings to her popular line of original Mini paintings. Over 25,000 of the mini paintings have been created and sold into art collections worldwide, and Jax holds a World Record for *The Most Original Acrylic Paintings on Canvas by One Artist.*

Jax is also the co-founder of the Women of Infinite Possibilities, an empowering women's organization started in Covington, LA. Jax can be found writing in her favorite local coffeehouse everyday with her loveable, tornado-of-a-pug named Lucy by her side.

Contact Jax for her available dates for book signings,
zoom meetings, and speaking engagements.
Sign up for the *Gumbeaux Sistahs* newsletter
at – www.gumbeauxsistahs.com
FB and Instagram – **Gumbeaux Sistahs**
Jax's art can be seen at: www.artbyjax.com
Facebook and Instagram; **Jax Frey**

WE LOVE REVIEWS!

Dear Readers:

Please share your reading experience of *The Gumbeaux Sistahs* novels:

- o Help others make good book choices
- o Help your authors get the word out about their work.

Simply leave a review of your favorite
Gumbeaux Sistahs *novel on Amazon.*

Here's how to leave a review:

- Just go to www.Amazon.com and search for T*he Gumbeaux Sistahs*
- Click on your favorite *Gumbeaux Sistahs* book title.
- Scroll down to find the "Review This Product" section to leave your review.

Here are some recent reviews to give you an example. The review can be long or short, it doesn't matter—they are all appreciated and helpful.

"I LOVED THIS BOOK. I CAN SO RELATE TO THIS BOOK. PEOPLE IN LOUISIANA ARE LIKE THIS. I can't wait to share this book with my own sistahs!"

"I absolutely LOVED this book, the style, and description of characters. I went on a cruise and read this book in 1 day! I couldn't put it down. GREAT book, especially if you know the area it takes place in. It's about community, helping one another out and just doing life together. A MUST read in your collection! Oprah needs to endorse it!! Just saying!"

"This is a great read for immersing yourself in the fun-loving, warmhearted, feel-good camaraderie that abounds in small Southern towns. The characters are quirky and interesting and find solutions to life's challenges over great gumbo and great wine. Just like my friends and me!"

And please copy and paste your Amazon review into your Facebook and Instagram accounts—thanks so very much for the Gumbeaux Sistah love! It helps so much.

OTHER BOOKS BY JAX FREY

The Gumbeaux Sistahs
(1st book in *Gumbeaux Sistahs* series)

Five fiery, Southern women wage a hilarious war against the problems of a sistah-in-trouble, using their improbable friendships, unpredictable schemes, oh-so-numerous cocktails, and a shared passion for good gumbo. *The Gumbeaux Sistahs* is a heart-warming, laugh-out-loud story you won't want to put down.

An official selection of the Pulpwood Queens—
the largest book club in the world with
over 800 book clubs registered.

Gumbeaux Love

(2nd book in the *Gumbeaux Sistahs* series)

Single, Southern artist Judith Lafferty casually confesses to her gumbeaux sistahs that she is occasionally lonely and would like to fall in love again. Seriously—you'd think that by now she would know to keep her mouth shut around these women. The sistahs tackle her problem along with their own love challenges with their usual unreasonable, extreme plots and schemes, including a kidnapping, a cupid costume, and trying out pick-up lines at the deli cheese counter. In helping out their friend, the sistahs help each other as well and bring to light the many flavors of love. Be ready for twists, turns, laugh-out-loud times, and heart-wrenching moments. You'll be sure to recognize yourself and your close friends in the unstoppable sistahs.

All *Gumbeaux Sistahs* novels are available at **Amazon.com** in paperback and kindle versions.
Order your signed paperback copies at www.gumbeauxsistahs.com

Coming Soon

More adventures with the
Gumbeaux Sistahs!

Sign up for the author newsletter to be the first to know when their next adventure is out at www.gumbeauxsistahs.com

Free Gift!

Sign up for Gumbeaux Sistahs newsletter to
receive a FREE, emailed, pdf version of

18 Gumbeaux Sistahs Steps to Living Happily Ever After

18 Steps that can change your life—try them today!
Visit www.gumbeauxsistahs.com and start
living happily ever after today!

READERS' GUIDE

THE GUMBEAUX SISTAHS
BY JAX FREY

1. *What three words would you use to best describe this book?*

2. *What was your favorite moment in the book? Your least favorite?*

3. *If you were in charge of casting the movie version of this book, who would you cast as each character?*

4. *If you could invite one character over to your house for dinner, who would it be & why?*

5. *If you had to trade places with any character in the book, who would you choose & why?*

6. *What surprised you the most when you were reading this book?*

7. *How did the setting of the book impact the story?*

8. *If you had to choose one lesson that the author was trying to teach us with this story, what would it be?*

10. *If you could write one more chapter after the ending, what would you write?*

Lucy says, "You look fabulous, sistah!"

www.ingramcontent.com/pod-product-compliance
Lightning Source LLC
Chambersburg PA
CBHW021314190726
48288CB00003B/842

* 9 7 8 1 7 3 3 1 5 8 2 2 0 *